# MEMORIES OF AN AUTUMN ROSE

## VILLES DES SAINTES

### BOOK ONE

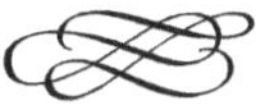

## JUDIE TROYANSKY

MEMORIES OF AN AUTUMN ROSE



ISBN:
Print: 978-0-9951544-4-5
E-Book: 978-0-9951544-5-2

Cover Artwork Designed by: Star Dragon Press
Photo of Death by: IngoLT from Adobe Stock Photo
Vectors for "Quilt Fabrics" by:
Creative Fabrica
Design Cuts
Vecteezy

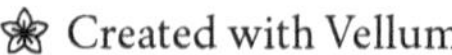 Created with Vellum

# ACKNOWLEDMENTS

Books have one author, but no one writes in a vacuum.

I'd like to thank my critique partners, Day's Lee, and Virginia Modugno for helping bring this book into the world. And an extra thank you to Virginia for her editing work. And Robin Patterson for her advice on the book's cover.

I'd also like to thank my long-time friends, Sandra Tickner-Broadhurst MA, Music Therapist, and Natalie Segal, MA, LCC, ADEC Member Thanatologist Loss and Grief Specialist, for their help in understanding grief.

And this novel wouldn't have been written without the support, caring, and occasional kick in the behind from my friends and family and the experiences we've shared.

Here's to making many more memories together.

# CONTENTS

"*I*t's my birthday." The little girl jumped in a circle on the bed, squealing with delight. Her auburn hair flew out in a halo. Her bare feet peeked out from beneath her long linen nightgown.

The Indian woman waited at the door, suppressing a smile.

"Tomorrow, my best little child. My *Beti*. You will be seven years old as soon as you wake up." The Indian woman adjusted the end of her red sari, throwing it over her shoulder.

"Do you think I can jump through the ceiling, Auntie-ji?" The child bounced and reached for the velvet canopy hanging above the bed.

"I don't think that is a good idea, my darling girl. It is raining outside. If you make a hole in the roof, this rug will be ruined, and it is such a pretty rug." The little girl stopped jumping and nodded solemnly. "Now, my dear little *Beti*, it is time for you to be in bed."

She jumped once more, landed on her seat, and scrambled under the down quilt.

The Indian woman looked out at the estate. The full moon cast shadows on the yew and rowan trees. The gamekeeper's lantern bobbed in the dark as he made his way back to his cottage. She closed the window curtains against the frosty country air.

"What story shall we have tonight then?" Auntie-ji smoothed the blankets over her charge and tucked her in.

Her little *Beti* smiled and toyed with the corner of the blanket.

"Oh no!" Auntie-ji put her hands together in prayer. "Not again."

*"Please?"* Beti bunched the blanket between her hands.

The Indian woman sighed and sat on the side of the bed. She turned away from the child's pleading expression. "No, no." She shook her head. "I know some nice stories with monkeys in them. Wouldn't you like a story about monkeys?"

Her *Beti* pouted, then whispered, "Please Auntie-ji?"

Auntie-ji glanced at her *Beti's* sad blue-gray eyes and quickly looked away. She distractedly rolled the carved ivory beads of her necklace between her fingers. The little girl took her hand, looking up at her through long lashes. Her expression was so forlorn. Auntie-ji could only sigh. "All right, all right." The little girl clapped her hands excitedly. Auntie-ji shook her head. "You know, *Beti*, I spoil you terribly, and no good will ever come of it."

*Beti* lay on her side, leaning on her elbow. "Once upon a time..."

"And who is telling this story?" Her gold bangles jingled as she folded her hands in her lap. "Once upon a time, in my country of India, a lovely English woman named Elizabeth wandered in the jungle far from her husband's home. In her arms, she carried her small baby. She didn't care that the jungle was dark. She didn't care that the jungle was full of dangers. She had a special duty to perform.

"You see Elizabeth had caught a sickness her people had never seen, and her time on Earth was coming to an end. And before her time was over, she wanted to find a special and important godparent for her baby daughter.

"The woman Elizabeth lived in dangerous times. The world was filled with soldiers and fighting and disease. She had to make sure there would be someone to care for her daughter when she was no longer there to take care of her.

"Elizabeth grew weary as the hour grew late. The strange howls of the jungle were all she heard over her own labored breathing. She drew strength from the fragrance of the night-blooming flowers and comfort from the soft, sleepy scent of the child in her arms. She rested against a tree, wiped her brow with the sleeve of her gown, and looked up into the star-filled sky.

"She called into the night, 'Is there no one in this whole world to whom I can entrust my baby?'

"Then, as easily as you or I can adjust the lamp, the moon changed position and shone at Elizabeth's feet. A voice as deep as the rumble of distant thunder spoke to her out of the moonlight.

"'Will I do?' said the voice."

The little girl sat up. "She heard the voice of God. Right Auntie-ji?"

"It was the voice of Jehovah, and he was asking to be the little girl's godparent. It was a great honor. Jehovah doesn't appear to just anyone anymore, let alone offer to help in such a plain-spoken manner.

"But this woman was not easily impressed. Elizabeth thought for a moment, and then she said, 'With all due respect Lord, you are far too busy to care for one small child. There are so many people praying to you, looking for answers, but you never seem to hear their prayers. You allow things to happen to unsuspecting people without warning and without reason. If you can't answer the prayers and pleas of all those people, how can you answer my daughter's questions when she is trying to find a lost toy?'

"She kissed her daughter, then looked up into the star-filled sky. 'Thank you for your consideration, but no thank You.' And with that, the moonlight faded, and the moon returned to its place in the sky."

The little girl moved closer to Auntie-ji and said, "Elizabeth called into the night again." She cupped her hands around her mouth and exhaled. "That was the warm breath she felt on the back of her neck."

"Would you like to tell this story?" Auntie-ji crossed her arms. The little girl shook her head. "Where was I?" Auntie-ji tapped her fore-finger against her lips. "Oh, yes. Elizabeth felt a warm breath on the back of her neck, and the air around her smelled of sulfur. When she turned around, there stood the Devil in all his finery. His suit was of royal velvet, and the buckles on his shoes were solid gold. On each of his fingers, he wore a diamond that sparkled like shooting stars in the night sky. Elizabeth had never seen such riches in her life.

"The Devil leaned on his ebony cane, looking too much like a cat that had used all of the farmer's cream to wash down a fresh young mouse. 'You were right not to choose him,' he said with a grin. 'I am by far the better choice.' He stroked his fine mustache. 'I have much I could teach the child, and she would never want for anything.'

"Did the Englishwoman accept the Devil's offer?" Auntie leaned toward her young charge.

"No!" The little girl slammed her fist onto the bed.

"She did not." The Indian woman straightened her spine. "Though she was ill, Elizabeth looked the Devil in the eye and said, 'Thank you, but you won't do at all.'"

"She was very brave, wasn't she, Auntie-ji?"

"Oh yes, *Beti*. She was very brave. But she remembered to say 'thank you' and to curtsy, for she had proper manners. 'Sir,' Elizabeth said, 'You may have fine clothes and jewels, but you are no gentleman. You lead good people into temptation, playing into their vanities and their greed, and you punish them for succumbing to your tricks.'

"Elizabeth kissed her daughter. 'I want my child to grow up to see past a person's wealth. I want her to grow up to help people. Again, sir, thank you for your consideration, but no.' The Devil laughed as he bowed to the Englishwoman and disappeared in a cloud of brimstone and smoke."

"And before Elizabeth lost hope, someone else appeared, right, Auntie-ji?"

"That's right." She patted the girl's hand. "It was a woman, but she was unlike anyone Elizabeth had ever seen.

"This woman was so terrible to look at, tears slipped down Elizabeth's cheeks. The woman's skirts were red with blood that continued to drip onto her bare feet. Her girdle was made from severed hands. Some still wore the rings of their previous owners. Her bare breasts were hidden behind a necklace of human skulls. Her skin was the blue of twilight. She held sharp swords in the hands of two of her eight arms. When she stepped forward, her anklets rang with the sound of distant, mournful cries.

"It was clear Elizabeth stood before a being of great power. She did not run away, even though she shook with awe."

"The baby's mother was very courageous to face such a powerful being, right, Auntie-ji?"

"She was more courageous than any tiger in any jungle in the whole world. Elizabeth curtsied to the fierce woman, looked her in the eye, and asked, 'Begging your pardon Madam, but who are you?'

"The fierce woman put away her swords and said, 'I am Kali Ma, the Goddess of Death.'

"The mother looked around the jungle, but she was all alone. 'Have you come for me so soon?' she asked.

"Kali shook her head. 'Not yet. But you will die a proud death, and I will be gentle when the time comes. I heard what you asked, and I am here at your request. I have come to be your baby's godmother.'

"'But you're Death,' Elizabeth said with surprise. She paused and thought for a moment. Then she slowly said, 'You are Death.' Elizabeth tilted her head and looked at the Goddess anew. 'You never discriminate between the rich or the poor, the good or the bad. You relieve the suffering of the ill and bring peace to the elderly.' Elizabeth smiled. 'Madam Kali Ma, thank you so much for coming. You are the perfect being to care for my daughter.'

"And there in the night, Kali Ma swore an oath by the sun, the moon, and all of the stars to care for the child named Autumn Rose."

"You forgot about the gift, Auntie-ji!"

"Oh, I would never forget about the gift. It's an important part of the story." She caressed her little *Beti*'s cheek. "Elizabeth let the Goddess hold the small infant. But Kali had never held a living human child before that night. Kali used the smallest part of her little finger to stroke the child's tiny fist. And do you know what Autumn Rose did?"

The girl nodded. "The baby grabbed Kali's finger."

"That's right. The little baby clutched her finger, and poor Kali was smitten. And so, as a gift, Kali promised to never take the child from Earth, to grant her immortality as long as the girl followed her godmother's instructions."

"And has the little girl been good?"

"Within reason and no more than can be expected." She stood up and tucked the blankets around the little girl. "But now it is time for my goddaughter to go to sleep." She kissed the child's forehead.

"Good night, my Auntie Kali."

"Good night, my Autumn Rose."

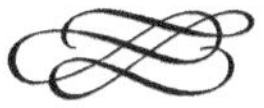

*G*one to get groceries had to be the most messed up suicide note in the history of the world.

Autumn Rose Sterling called out to her husband, Eddie, but the small cottage was quiet. When he didn't answer, she wrote the note.

Rose put on some lipstick, so she looked less pale. She wasn't *really* going to kill herself. Taking the car keys from her purse, she closed the door quietly behind her. She was going to ask her godmother for a little help.

Rose looked back at the house and sighed. She tightened the belt on her coat. It, like most of her clothes, was too big now. Their car was in the driveway, but she went toward the backyard instead. The trees around the lake had started to change color, their hues reflected in the still water. She had always wanted to paint this view, to make it into a woven tapestry, or an embroidery pattern. Maybe next time.

Rose pulled her pendant out from beneath her sweater. She clasped it in her hand and said a prayer to Kali Ma, the Hindu Goddess of Death.

"Auntie-ji, I need your help. I have cancer. Please help me end this life with dignity." She took a photograph of her family from her coat pocket. Her granddaughter had taken it last summer. Zoe had used the timer, so she, Rose, Eddie, and their daughter Nora could all be in the photo together. It was Rose's new favorite. "Everything is ready. Eddie and Nora know everything. Well, not *everything* everything. But Eddie has agreed to be Autumn's guardian when she gets here." She watched the sunlight reflect off the water.

"Auntie-ji, I'm scared, but I don't want to spend my final days in the hospital." The weariness was taking its toll. "I don't want to end my days in a sterile, featureless room. Away from all this beauty and art. I couldn't bear seeing the look of hopelessness in Eddie's eyes. I want him to remember all the fun we had together. I want Nora to remember me laughing with her at the gallery. And I want Zoe to remember me finger painting and crafting hats with her. I don't want them to remember me as a bald old woman who needs someone to connect her feeding tube because she might choke on a glass of water. In all my other cycles, I only lived until 60. I passed that ten years ago. It's time. Please, Auntie-ji?"

Rose looked up at the sky, waiting for some kind of reply. There was no sudden rainbow or crash of thunder. The sky was still clear; the breeze was still gentle. She sighed, hoping Kali had heard.

Rose started the car's engine. The classic Mustang roared to life. The gravel of the country road kicked out behind the tires as she veered onto the highway.

Rose wouldn't be at Rowan House, their home in Ville des Saintes, this evening. She wouldn't be at Sterling's Fine Art and Whatnot Gallery on Tuesday either. She hated this. She hated having to make this decision. But there was no turning back for Rose now. Why had it been so much easier before?

Rose watched the scenery flow past the windshield. The colors of fall blanketed the hills. Tones of russet and gold covered the landscape like a quilt. The sky was a cyan blue. The clouds were lacy and white with undertones of silver and lilac.

"Where are we going?" Eddie sat up in the back seat. Rose's heart jumped into her mouth as she swerved the car back into her lane.

"What are you doing there?" Rose said. "I told you I was just going to get some groceries."

"I thought I'd come with." Eddie leaned his cheek against the top of the passenger seat.

Rose looked around. They'd already started the climb into the hills. There was no place to pull over and let Eddie out. "I wish you hadn't come."

"Why? You were only planning on shopping." He didn't wait for her to answer. "But it wasn't shopping that you were planning at all, was it? You don't need to do this. Let's just go home, Rosie."

"It's not that easy." She wiped tears from her eyes. "You weren't supposed to be here. I needed to do this alone."

"But I promised to take care of you. Through sickness, and in health."

"This is about what I need to do for you. No hospitals. No wasting into nothing."

"I understand everything." He put his hand on her shoulder. "We'll find another way, Rosie. Forget about groceries. Let's go to the pub. We'll have a good dinner, and we'll talk."

A silver Rolls-Royce passed them on the two-lane highway. A dark-haired woman sat in the back seat. The sign she'd been waiting for. This was it.

Rose covered Eddie's hand with her own. Eddie Sterling. Her true love. Her husband of fifty years. They loved each other more today than when they were first married.

Eddie had left a CD of his favorite music from the '60s in the player. It was special because their granddaughter had made it for him. Blood, Sweat, and Tears played one of their most popular songs about the spinning wheel, spinning. Eddie started singing along, tapping a rhythm out on the seat. Normally, Rose would sing too, but today it felt like someone had poured cold water over her heart.

"Eddie, I don't know what to say. You weren't supposed to be here. You were supposed to be home. Safe."

"But Rose, we're only going into the village. To the pub."

"It's our last dance, my darling. I am so, so sorry."

"What are you talking about?"

Rose saw a small image of Kali floating above the dashboard. There was a sharp pain in her chest. Her breath caught in her throat. "Forgive me, my love." Her body was no longer connected to her mind.

Eddie was calling her name. She could hear the tears in his voice. The steering wheel turned in her hand. Eddie couldn't grab the wheel from the back seat. The sunlight was fading. The edges of her vision were going dark. The highway twisted around the mountain. Tires squealed around the first turn. The car hit the rail, metal scraping against metal, spinning around as the guard rail gave way.

They were falling, falling. Eddie screamed her name. She tried to speak but couldn't. Rolling over and over. *Spinning Wheel* still played through the car's speakers. Her purse bounced off the windshield, and the ceiling. The small clasp broke on impact. Keys and eyeglasses, spare change, and store receipts rained down upon them. The car flipped twice more before it slid to a stop.

Eddie's eyes were closed. His cheeks were cut, bleeding, and raw. She tried to call to him, but her words slurred, and she had no feeling in her arm. The pain shot down her back and through her legs. It hurt to breathe. They were far from town and far from home. She felt Eddie take her hand.

She closed her eyes, and the pain faded.

"Autumn Rose, can you hear us?" The voice sounded sweet. She'd heard it before. Auntie-ji's friends? The Three Fates?

"Lachesis, do you think she knows we're here?"

"I think she does, Clotho." The second woman's voice was deeper and had a calming quality to it. "Rose. It's time, my dear. Autumn Rose, you have to tell us what you want."

"Can she change her mind?" Clotho asked.

An older woman answered, a slight tremor in her voice. "Of course she can. She has free will."

"Atropos," Clotho said, "I don't think she can hear us. How will we know if she's changed her mind? I don't think she knows we're here."

"She knows," Lachesis said. "She always knows how to call to us."

Rose sensed a face close to hers. The breath cooling her cheek smelled of peppermint. "It's Atropos, child. Just tell us what you want, my dear. The spark is ready for you. We will do whatever you say."

Rose wasn't sure if she had spoken. She wanted them to tell her about Eddie. She wanted to cry. She couldn't move. She couldn't see. Sirens. Metal crunching and a mechanical whine. A helicopter. And all the while *Spinning Wheel* kept playing on the radio.

Hands reached for her. Rough hands. Gloved hands. Ghost hands. Pulling her away from the car. Away from Eddie. Away from her life.

"*H*ey, Zoe!"

Zoe Williams turned and snapped a photo of Taylor Main gazing lovingly into the eyes of a marble angel. Taylor had got heavily into researching the 1920s, just in case the 2020s were roaring too. Everything about her style choices this semester shouted, *silent film diva*. Taylor's straight black hair had been cut into a bob with bangs and her makeup played up her eyes. Today she wore a cloche hat and a long cloth coat over her jeans.

Zoe breathed in the crisp fall air. A graveyard was a stupid place to hold an art class. She ignored the shiver running up her spine, zipped the camera case back into her knapsack, and put her arms through the straps.

Some of her friends passed by, nodding hello. First day back at school. Her mom told her not to expect much. Some people wouldn't know what to say, some people just wouldn't know it had happened. At least she had Taylor. She'd just be Taylor, so Zoe could just be Zoe. Zoe the art student. Not the Zoe whose grandparents died tragically in a car accident.

Her challenge today was to just be normal, like nothing had

happened. Like she hadn't missed close to a month of school. Taylor would help.

Smile Zoe. Play your part. "You know Taylor, your taste in boys has always been questionable." She tilted her head toward the marble statue. "But I think you've outdone yourself with that one."

"Oh, I don't know." Taylor twirled her long-beaded necklace as she swayed down the walk, playing it up so that she looked more like a model on a New York runway and less like a high school student on a path in a cemetery. "Sure, he might be a bit cold, but he doesn't argue or notice other girls, and I always know where he's hanging out."

Zoe smirked. Taylor batted her eyes. "Now, let me see." She pulled Zoe's camera toward her. "It definitely has potential. You put it up on Insta-chat. I'm going to put it up on FriendlyFaces."

"Why not just post it on both?"

"Because I can't always post about me. My friends have to show some love too, you know." Taylor fell silent for a moment as she studied the image. "We'll call it, *Hashtag Divine!* And don't forget the exclamation mark, okay? I might even use it as my new profile picture. The one there is at least a week old."

They heard the voices of some of the other students in their art class above the sounds of the sparse afternoon traffic. Zoe started scanning the rest of the photos on the card, landscapes of downtown Ville des Saintes. Some random people prepared for Halloween, while others next door got ready for Christmas.

There were photos of her grandparents. The camera had been a birthday gift from them, something to replace the old point-and-shoot she'd inherited from her father after his last upgrade. Her mother, Grandma Rose, and Grandpa Eddie had all hammed it up, so she could practice using the different camera settings. They all laughed so hard. Grandma found some old hats and clothes in the attic, and they roamed all over her grandparents' mansion, posing. They almost made her forget that her father had forgotten her birthday and missed his weekly visitation call from Hong Kong—again.

Here was a photo of her grandparents with half-closed eyes and puckered lips, a pose they had copied from a selfie Zoe had posted of herself and Taylor. She had used the photo to explain modern photography and that peace signs were no longer in fashion. Grandma Rose obliged, but Grandpa Eddie still held up two fingers.

This one had Grandma Rose leaning back against the kitchen counter, her arms supporting her weight on the counter behind her, her chin high, her eyes skyward. She said she was posing like the legendary Theda Bara. Zoe had to look up who she was. Her mom wasn't sure who she was either, except her name showed up often in crossword puzzles.

"Zo-weeeee," Taylor whined. "You're not listening."

When Zoe explained to her grandparents she was going to use some of the camera's built-in filters, her grandparents conspired to kiss—just to weird her out. In the sepia-toned photo, Grandpa's eyes were closed, but Grandma's were open. When Zoe asked, Grandma Rose said she never wanted to miss a minute with her husband. The last picture was an experiment with the timer settings, a black-and-white of her, her mother, and her grandparents. The hospital found a copy of the photo in her grandmother's coat pocket after the accident.

Taylor peeked over her shoulder at the viewscreen. Zoe smiled, tears in her eyes.

Taylor hugged her. "Please don't. You'll get me started, and we'll both end up with mascara running down our faces. It's too early in the semester to go raccoon without being a goth."

Zoe took a deep breath, pasted on a smile, and saved the photos to her cloud account. "Okay, Taylor. You have my full attention. We are back in the moment."

"How very Zen of you." Taylor straightened her shoulders. "As I was saying... Let's skip this dead-fest and head downtown."

"We can't." Zoe twisted her curly auburn hair up into a bun and secured it with a clip. "First, it's Special Projects, so there are only ten of us in the class, and second, the notes I got were from Ms. Flowers. I haven't even met the new teacher yet."

"She hasn't met anyone yet. And she's only giving out the assignment today. You're golden."

"Not really. My mother is unveiling my grandparents' headstone at the beginning of December. The week will be totally lost to my own work. I have to get ahead of the assignment if I expect to get it in on time."

"And you won't get any time off?"

"I'll have to be available to smile and pretend I recognize all of my grandparents' old friends and clients." She patted Taylor's cheek and spoke in a thick New York accent. "Zoe, babydoll. You've gotten so tall. Do you remember me? Of course you do. You don't? Oy, darling —don't worry about it. I'm not offended. After all, the last time I was in town, you were two."

Taylor laughed. "Seriously?" Zoe raised her eyebrows, *an honest-to-God* look on her face. Taylor pointed at a black marble slab with the name of the deceased encircled by incised forget-me-knots. "So why is there going to be such a fuss about one of those?"

"Because my grandparents' headstone is being created by Thomas Paloma, the sculptor whose *Dog with Boy and Alligator* sold for just under two million dollars."

Taylor swallowed. "Two million? Do you have a hunk of rock and a chisel I can borrow?"

Zoe smiled. "And he's doing it as a gift."

Taylor rocked on her heels and batted her eyes. "Could you mention to him that *my* birthday is coming up?"

"Grandpa Eddie gave him his first show back in the '80s when he was still actually carving headstones for a living." She paused and watched a double-decker tour bus lumber down the roadway outside the cemetery. "My mother has planned these amazing exhibitions in honor of Rose and Eddie's fiftieth wedding anniversary and Sterling's Fine Art and Whatnot's fortieth year in business. The gallery's hosting a retrospective of the work of *The Crayon Box Collective*, and the fine art museum is going to show work by all the other Canadian artists my grandparents discovered or mentored."

"It sounds like it's going to be an amazing event."

"The shows were supposed to be for their double anniversary celebration. Now it's going to be their memorial."

"Why didn't your mom just cancel?" Taylor used her cell phone's camera as a mirror and applied another coat of lip gloss.

"Because it took almost two years to get everything set up. On the bright side, at least their deaths didn't mess up the opening."

"Well, aren't you just a bundle of sunshine and unicorn farts. Did your evil stepmother hide your gown for the ball?" Taylor shook out her black hair, and pursed her lips, posing for her newest selfie.

"Rose and Eddie loved a great party. They loved having their friends and family around them. They loved supporting the city's museums and introducing people to great art and artists. But none of this is for them. They can't enjoy any of it. They're dead." Zoe could feel her chest begin to tighten. Breathe in for the count of four. Slowly exhale for the count of four. The anger and anxiety would calm down eventually. She could feel Taylor watching her, waiting. "I'm good."

"You will be. I promise." Taylor put her arm around Zoe's shoulders.

"Let's get down to business." Taylor took Zoe's hand and linked their arms. "Alas, while Ms. Flowers is currently enjoying her newly adopted daughter, we must suffer a teacher who has no history at the school." Zoe let herself be led toward their classmates. "Let's go meet our new taskmaster."

They rounded the corner and stopped short. A tall Black woman stood on the path. Her skin's rich sepia could only be achieved by master photographers. She wore her long hair in multiple braids, which looped back onto themselves and cascaded down her back. Large gold beads decorated her hair. She wore a long brocade coat over a gold turtleneck sweater, skinny jeans, and knee-high leather boots. Zoe hoped her mouth wasn't hanging open. The woman turned to look at the girls and smiled a smile so warm and welcoming, that Zoe felt she'd known this woman all her life.

The woman waved them forward. "Ladies and gentlemen, welcome to the all-encompassing major assignment you'll need to pass to move on to your senior year." She spoke with a Jamaican accent. "While it is in your agenda as Special Projects, it has been christened by those who have passed this way before you as *The Circle of Hell Dante Forgot to Write About."* She handed a stack of papers to the closest student and asked him to pass them around. "My name is Oya Bridges, and I will be your adviser, facilitator, mother-confessor, and lifeline through this assignment."

Ms. Bridges scanned the paper in her hand. "As you can see, the photos and artwork will be due at the end of the month, so the installation can be mounted for December 3rd."

Taylor whispered, "Isn't that the same week as your mom's event?"

Zoe chewed the inside of her cheek. The dentist had warned her about grinding her teeth on her last visit.

"Scrapbooks, notes, and papers must be in my office by the day's end on December 15th. We'll discuss the opening of the exhibit when we go over the details of mounting the show in Sterling Hall."

Zoe read the paper while Ms. Bridges continued talking about the history of Snowy Hill Cemetery and the historical figures buried there. It truly was a morbid assignment.

*"Grade 10—Visual Arts and Decorative Arts Joint Presentation*

*Essay: THE STORY OF A LIFE.*

*Find a monument (headstone) for a famous or infamous resident of Snowy Hill Cemetery. Note the person's name, date of birth, and date of death. Photograph the monument, remembering to pay attention to the points of composition discussed with Ms. Flowers earlier. These include the rule of thirds, leading lines, lighting, background elements, and points of focus.*

*Once your photos have been taken, begin researching what the world would have looked like during your resident's lifetime: things they would have worn, modes of transportation, headlines from the era, etc. Include elements of their lives and what made their time in Ville des Saintes special. If your subject is a known historical figure, you will be responsible for verifiable facts and biographical accuracy.*

*Speak to other members of the class and see if any of your periods overlap. Should this happen, please feel free to work on certain aspects of your installations together."*

The group broke up. Some of the students headed back into the cemetery while others stayed to ask questions about the assignment.

Taylor lay her head on Zoe's shoulder. "And who are you doing your project on? As if I didn't know."

"Harvey Workman." Zoe shouldered her bag and headed toward the path to the pond. "I remember his last exhibit. His stuff is amazing. He's buried in the Jewish section."

"Wait a minute." Taylor stepped in front of Zoe, blocking her. "You're not doing the project on either of your grandparents? They're buried here, right?"

"But they don't have a monument, and they won't have one until after the due date."

"I think Ms. Bridges would understand."

"I don't want to do my project on them. Harvey Workman was one of the founders of *The Crayon Box Collective*. He's the person I'm doing my project on."

"But your grandmother had all of those scrapbooks and letters. The paper would practically write itself." Taylor sighed. "The school's gallery was donated by your grandparents. Their pictures are in the entryway. Their last name is in big gold letters above the door."

"I'm not doing the project on their lives. Because. I. Don't. Want. To!" Zoe growled, then pushed past Taylor. She could follow behind or not. Zoe didn't care.

Zoe had to pass in front of the rest of the class to get to the path. Before she could get through the mingling students, Ms. Bridges called to her. Zoe whispered a swear word and went over to the bench where Ms. Bridges was holding court. The other students fell away, leaving them alone on the bench.

"I heard about the passing of your grandparents. I'm very sorry for your loss." Zoe never knew how to respond, so she just nodded. "Your grandparents were big supporters of the community and champions of artists everywhere. If you want to do your project on their lives, you have my full support. They were lovely people, and I feel learning about their history will give you a deeper understanding of them as people and as artists, see them beyond just being your grandparents."

At least she didn't use the word *closure* or mention *the tragedy of their loss*. Zoe mumbled, "I'll think about it."

Zoe turned and walked up the hill. She crumpled the assignment into a ball and shoved it into her pocket. She didn't need some stupid school project to tell her about her grandparents. She knew everything there was to know about her grandparents. Unlike her parents and their divorce-by-whisper campaign, her grandparents never kept secrets. "Talk and tell it like it is," was Grandpa Eddie's life motto.

Those shady jackasses on the school's board just wanted access to her grandparents' archives so they could cash in on all the visitors coming to the two retrospectives. They had been calling her mother at home and at work, even before the accident, to get stuff for the Sterling Hall gallery so they would be included in the program and advertising the Ville des Saints Heritage Committee was putting together. And she just became their way in.

Zoe had been at Sterling Hall for its dedication two years ago and had helped Grandma Rose cut the ribbon. Her grandparents loved art, but they loved her more, and they had been at the head of the line for her first show. No, her second show. Her grandparents had mounted her first show.

She'd only been nine when she fell in love with photography. Zoe was twelve when her parents divorced. It was not long after that, Zoe's father decided to sell the family's home out from under them. And her mother needed help moving them out of their house. They had the condo left to her mother by Grandpa Eddie's parents. Her father had wanted to sell it when they had bought the house in Summit Woods, but her mother refused—and it was a good thing, too.

To help keep Zoe occupied, Eddie and Rose had come up with things to keep their granddaughter busy. They brought her to the gallery to help with paper shredding and document stapling, paying her five dollars an hour for her work.

When she became curious about how they chose paintings and artwork for an exhibit, they said they would help her create her first one-woman show. They sent her out with their driver, Uncle Theo. She'd spent two months of summer vacation photographing every place she loved being. She sat every evening with Grandpa Eddie, discussing and choosing her favorite photos from the hundreds she'd taken. When everything was complete, Grandma Rose put her photos into frames, and together with Grandpa Eddie and, her mother, Nora, they removed all the artwork and furniture from their living room.

Grandpa Eddie hung every photo for her exhibition. Grandma Rose made sure it was all done right. They served grape juice, and apple juice in plastic wine glasses, and cookies were brought through the crowd on gold trays by white-gloved staff, just like at Grandpa Eddie's Harbor Front gallery. She even had small adhesive dots to put on the photos which sold. And there was a crowd, her grandparents made sure of it. They invited all their friends who were in town and some of her school friends, and everyone behaved as if it were a real gallery opening. And she loved them for it.

Zoe stopped to catch her breath and figure out in which direction she was supposed to be going. She looked out over the sea of head-stones. All those lives—ended. Their stories were over. Did any of them ever get their happily ever after? Or were they just…gone? Just over. Just like Grandpa Eddie and Grandma Rose.

There was no reason for her grandparents to have died. Grandma Rose shouldn't have been driving. Grandpa Eddie shouldn't have let her. She was starting to get better. Why didn't she realize something was off? She should have told someone she wasn't feeling well. They had Uncle Theo. He was their driver. Why hadn't they let him drive?

A flock of Canada geese honked past, but Zoe refused to look up and try to find their 'V'. That was a Grandma Rose thing. A thing they used to do together. She had only one wish for them to carry with them; she wanted to see her grandparents just once more. She closed her eyes, immediately feeling the hopelessness of it all. It was a silly and childish thing to do anyway. Stupid geese. Stupid wind making her eyes tear. And no stupid tissue in her stupid pocket.

Zoe felt a hand on her shoulder. Taylor held out a pack of tissues. "Thanks," Zoe mumbled.

"Anyone interesting in Harvey Workman's neighborhood?"

"Ms. Bridges wants me to do my project on Grandpa Eddie."

"Well, Ms. Bridges can go screw herself." She put an arm around

Zoe's shoulder. "Just add a line like, 'Harvey Workman founded *The Crayon Box Collective* with Edward Sterling.' End of story."

"I could do that, couldn't I?" Zoe smiled. "And I'm sure we can find someone interesting for you. There are a couple of actors and an author or two not far from where we're going."

"Anyone scandalous?"

"We'll make sure of it."

*T*aylor flipped the map sideways. "I definitely, for sure, know where we are."

"Where?" Zoe walked in a circle, her smartphone high in the air.

"We're in the Snowy Hill Cemetery." Zoe's eyeroll spoke volumes. Taylor folded the map. "Still no signal?"

"Nothing." Zoe lowered her arms.

"We're in the middle of the city. How can there be no cell reception?"

"I guess they take the whole *rest in peace* thing seriously." Zoe held her hand out. Taylor gave her the map. "The map says the place has three gates, and they're all at the base of the hill. So, I suggest we keep heading downhill. If we don't come to a gate, we'll follow the wall until we find one."

"That's okay for the gates on the downtown side, but what happens if we end up on King Street?" They started walking again.

"If we end up on King, we'll just call..." She was going to say she'd call her grandmother. Whenever she spent all her bus fare, or had too many packages, or she wanted to visit the family at the gallery, she'd call Grandma Rose. And Uncle Theo would appear, just like magic.

Taylor put her arm around Zoe's shoulder. "I wouldn't mind seeing the Bentley right about now, either."

They rounded the corner and spotted what looked like her grandparents' car. Just like magic. Zoe looked up at the path marker. They weren't lost. Zoe knew where they were.

A man walked back to the car and leaned against the hood. Even from this distance, she recognized Uncle Theo's heavy build and straight black hair. A woman in a red sari was standing beside him.

"We're saved!" Zoe smiled and quickened her pace.

"Zoe, wait. What are they doing here?"

"I haven't seen Uncle Theo since forever. I'm sure he and his friend won't mind giving us a ride home." Zoe turned to walk backward. "Or they can take us back to Rowan House, and we can make some tea." She turned back toward the car. "He could help us with our project too. Whenever someone came to visit, they..." Zoe froze in her tracks. She stopped rambling. She stopped smiling. She felt like she'd stopped breathing.

Uncle Theo and the Indian woman were laying flowers on her grandparents' graves. Her grandparents were there. In the ground. They would be there forever now.

Then she remembered the sound. That horrible, hollow, echoing sound of shovelfuls of dirt hitting the wooden coffins. Zoe started to shake. The sound had been in her nightmares. Rose and Eddie weren't going to be in the Bentley. They would never be at Rowan House again. They were never coming home.

"Look, Zoe, over there. It's Ms. Bridges." Taylor took her friend's hand, just like she'd done on their first day of kindergarten. "Come on. Let's get out of here. It's freezing." Taylor led her away from the graves and back toward their teacher. "We'll head downtown and have some hot chocolate. I'm buying... unless I forgot my wallet. Not even a small sarcastic remark? Well, this means my only choice now is..."

Zoe let herself be led away. She couldn't hear anything Taylor said. The sound of her heart breaking was just too loud.

*Z*oe carried a tray holding ceramic mugs of hot chocolate. Taylor held the plates of brownies. The café was filled with students from their school and from McCord University. They were lucky and found a booth. The university's library was across the street, and most of the university's students ran on caffeine.

"Do you want to talk about it?" Taylor asked as she slid onto the bench opposite Zoe. "Or we can talk about something else?"

"My mother is the only family I have left. I mean, blood family. You and I are sisters forever. But... you know what I mean."

Taylor nodded. Zoe sighed as she stirred her hot chocolate. "I have my mother. But my father and his new family live in Hong Kong. I can count on one hand the number of times I've spoken to him in the last year. My mom called to tell him what happened to Rose and Eddie. But she was boiling mad by the time she got off the phone."

"Looking for a cut of the estate?" Taylor asked. Zoe nodded. "Heart of gold, your father."

"Not possible. If he had one, the step-monster would have sold it by now." Zoe traced patterns in a small puddle of hot chocolate with her stir stick.

"Hello, ladies," Joshua Kempt, Taylor's ex-boyfriend, and his twin brother Jacob stood beside their table. "May we join you?"

"What do you want, Joshua?" Taylor said, not giving up any space on the bench. She put her foot beside Zoe so she couldn't move over either.

"We're taking numbers for the special project," Jacob said.

"Phone numbers?" asked Zoe.

"No. We are selling lottery numbers," Jacob said. "Only two bucks."

"It's for a very special drawing," Joshua continued. "To see which lucky artist should be allowed to work with us and propose to Ms. Bridges we be allowed to do our project on the Sterlings. Let's face it, anyone who does their project on them will be awarded prime gallery space, even if they paint stick figures on kids' construction paper."

"It's an easy *A*, plus you'd get your name in the paper. All the glory without any of the work," Jacob said.

"We'll be the stars. The others will be like satellites, basking in our greatness." Joshua smiled. "Jacob and I have an in. Our uncle used to work at their gallery."

"What's his name?" Zoe asked.

"Walter Kempt. He worked there when they first opened on the Harbor Front," said Jacob. "But we wouldn't want to ruin anyone else's chances. So, we thought we'd raffle off the privilege of working on our project."

Taylor looked at Zoe, who was picking stray icing off the edge of her plate. Taylor smiled innocently. "I guess your uncle has a lot of photos and things about the Sterlings?"

"Not much, but he has a lot of stories about them and *The Crayon Box Collective*." Zoe's hand tightened around her mug. Jake continued. "He's ready to tell everything he knows. Things like the wild parties he attended at their mansion, and how they used to do drugs on the back lawn. All kinds of juicy stuff like that."

Joshua winked suggestively.

Zoe broke the wooden stir stick into tiny pieces. "I hope you haven't sold a lot of tickets. You're going to have to give everyone their money back." She looked the twins in the face. "See, it's too late. I'm already doing my project on the Sterlings. Ms. Bridges approached me and personally asked me to do the assignment. And that's that."

"And what makes you so special?" Joshua said, his voice dripping with sarcasm.

Zoe wished she had a flamethrower, so she could melt the twins together. Then they might have one complete brain, instead of the half-brain genetics had awarded each of them. "It could be because I'm a better artist than the two of you put together. Or it could be because I won't embarrass the school by taking the contents of my locker, piling it in the middle of the gallery floor, and call it an installation. Or maybe I was chosen because Rose and Edward Sterling are my grandparents."

"Yeah, right." The twins rolled their eyes in concert.

"It's true," Taylor said. "All of it."

"Fine." Jacob pulled out his smartphone. "Prove it." He ran a search on his phone. His finger hovered over the *dial* button. "We'll just call their gallery and find out who's telling the truth. It's called Sterling Fine Art and Whatnot, you know."

"Wait a minute. What do we get if we're telling the truth?" Taylor asked.

"Our undying devotion," said Joshua.

"I'd prefer cash," Taylor said.

Joshua and Jacob compared wallets. "We've got twenty between us," Jacob said. "You?"

The girls put their heads together and whispered.

"They're idiots." Zoe side-eyed the twins.

Taylor batted her eyes, a sweet smile on her face. "And that's why we should let them give us their money."

"We shouldn't take money from them because they're idiots," Zoe said. "It's like we have an unfair advantage."

"If you're afraid of being found out..." Joshua smiled condescendingly. "We won't tell anyone about this conversation. Well, not all of it, anyway. Just the part about you being afraid of losing twenty dollars and..."

"You're on," Zoe said. "Dial away."

Jacob hit the dial button, put his phone on speaker, and lay it on the table between them. The phone rang a few times. A woman answered, "Sterling Harbor Front. Nora Sterling speaking. How can I help you?"

"Are you related to Edward and Rose Sterling?" Jacob asked.

"I'm their daughter. Is there something I can help you with?"

"Hi Mom." Zoe smiled at the boys.

"Hi sweetie. What's up?"

"Taylor and I were having a bite at Timmies."

The twins looked at each other and grew a bit pale.

"Hi Aunt Nora," Taylor said.

"Hi Taylor. How's everyone?"

"Everyone's good."

"Please tell your mother yoga class is still happening on Thanksgiving Monday. We'll have to leave a bit early though. Parking in the area is going to be brutal."

"I'll tell her about the yoga."

"Anyway," Zoe continued, "it turns out two of our classmates said their uncle worked at the gallery after they moved to the harbor. Would you remember him? His name's Walter Kempt."

"They moved the gallery in the early '80s. Which means I was about ten."

"So, you don't remember him?"

Nora paused. "I wasn't at the gallery much, back then. I remember some of the people who worked here at the time. I've met some of the old-timers over the years too. But most, I just know about from your grandfather's stories." There was a shuffling of paper. "You said his name was Walter Kempt?"

"Yes." Jacob leaned closer to the phone. "K-E-M-P-T."

"Give me a minute." They heard her type something. "I looked at the birthday calendar. No one at the gallery named Kempt."

Taylor looked at Zoe, her eyebrows asking the question. "My grandparents kept a calendar with the birthdays and anniversaries of everyone who ever worked at the gallery, their best clients, and the artists they represented. They would send cards or phone people, just to keep in touch."

"Wait a minute. If I remember correctly, my dad used to tell this story about a high school kid who used to walk Pippin. I think his name was Wally... I guess that could have been your Uncle Walter."

"Pippin?" Zoe said.

"Do you remember Mrs. Shine, the bookkeeper? She retired about five years ago. She once had this yappy poodle mix named Pippin. Wally used to come by after school and walk the dog."

"Aunt Nora, was Walter ever at Rowan House?"

"Why would he be at our house?" Nora laughed. "We didn't have a dog."

"Thanks, Mom. I'll see you later."

"Wait. Aunt Nora?" Taylor smiled smugly at Joshua. "What was the story your father used to tell?"

"Well, there was this time Wally showed up at the gallery to walk the dog. It seems Wally had taken his first painting class and fancied himself an artist. My parents were great with art students, no matter what their age. They'd stand in front of a painting and point out everything from the texture created by the brush strokes to the depth of the shadows. But Wally decided he knew everything. He stood in the office holding Pippin's leash while he harshly critiqued every piece of art hanging in the gallery."

"Sounds like Uncle Walter," Jacob whispered to his brother, getting an elbow in the ribs for his trouble.

Nora continued. "My father was very patient, according to my mother. When Wally finally came up for air, my dad said he'd find the paper towels in the bathroom. It seemed, during Wally's monologue, Pippin had taken the opportunity to pee on his shoes."

Taylor burst out laughing.

Zoe giggled, "Thanks, Mom. I'll see you at home."

"Bye, my two sweeties."

"He never worked at the gallery." Taylor chuckled. "He was the bookkeeper's dog walker and fire hydrant. Real strong connection there dude. Maybe you should see if they all went to the same dentist too."

The boys gave each other accusing looks as they started digging the money out of their wallets, piling the bills and coins between the girls. "Good luck on your project."

Joshua turned on the charm. "Do you need a partner? After all, you had two grandparents."

"Thanks," said Zoe. "But Taylor has already agreed to work with me on this."

Taylor paused as she pushed half their winnings toward Zoe. "I have? Yes, I have." Taylor smiled at the twins. "I'm working on the Sterlings for the assignment." She swept the money into her purse. "And thanks for the hot chocolate."

# TUESDAY, OCTOBER 2ND, 2017

*A*utumn Rose's eyes popped open, her heart hammering against her chest. The car. Turning over and over. Such horrible deaths.

She stared at the ceiling of her bedroom. Still the same fancy plaster flowers encircling the light fixture. Still the same warm flannel duvet. Still two pillows behind her head, just the way she liked.

"Breathe," she whispered to herself. "Just breathe. It was just a nightmare. You're safe." She glanced around the room without lifting her head. "See? All of your stuff is here."

There was a knock at the door. "*Beti*? May I come in?" Kali stood in the doorway. She wore Autumn's favorite purple and gold sari. Her string of carved bone beads hung around her neck. "Is everything all right?"

"Yes Auntie-ji. I'm fine." Autumn sat up and threw off the blankets. "I just had a nightmare," she said to herself as well as Kali.

Kali came into the room and handed Autumn a mug. "A bad dream? What was it about?"

Autumn thanked Kali for the tea and took a sip. "It was strange. This man and woman were riding in this car, traveling through the mountains. I was the woman in the car. We had been married for about fifty years, and we had a grandchild. He was old. I was old." She crossed her legs. "In the dream, we were headed someplace… I don't remember where we were, just somewhere we liked to go. Suddenly, I got sick. Like I was having a stroke or something. The car goes off the road, and we die."

"A dream?" Kali seemed surprised. "That was quite detailed for a dream."

"But I'm not old. I'm seventeen. At least I will be at the end of the month." Autumn paused. "The car was one of those classic sports cars."

"What else do you remember about the people from this dream?"

"Not much." Autumn shrugged.

Kali held her hand out for the mug, but Autumn still held on to it. "I think the best cure for a bad dream is to get out of bed and focus on the present," Kali said. "Don't you remember? We still have to open the house. Rose had many of the rooms closed when she became ill."

Autumn nodded. She didn't remember anything about the house. She couldn't remember anything that had happened yesterday. She couldn't even remember getting into bed last night. Who was Rose? That was the name of the woman in the dream. Was this her house? Was she somehow related?

Kali sighed. "We don't have time for wool-gathering, *Beti*. Everything is upside down and not where it's supposed to be. Your purse and wallet are in the closet, but you have to apply for a new passport. I found some of your clothing, but I had to send Thanatos to get new toiletries. I will have everything you need to start your day by the time you have finished your shower."

The Grim Reaper, whose picture was on the tarot card *Death*, was part of the household and acted as their driver. It was funny to think of Thanatos—Uncle Theo—in his professional gear, scyth on his shoulder, walking through the pharmacy, choosing deodorant and toothpaste. At least she remembered him.

Kali held her hand out again. Autumn quickly finished the tea and gave her godmother the mug. Kali made her way to the door. "*Beti*, I'm sorry. I forget sometimes you're only a human and all of this can be very disorienting. Don't worry. Everything will seem familiar again in no time."

Once Kali closed the door, Autumn got off the bed. The nightmare still clung to the air like a man's aftershave. She recognized this room. She just couldn't remember how she got here or where she'd been before.

Someone was watching her. She felt their eyes on the back of her neck. Autumn scanned the shadows. Stupid nightmares.

$A$utumn stepped out of the shower and wrapped herself in the big fluffy towel Kali had left warming on the rack. She used the side of her hand to wipe the steam from the mirror.

She stared at her face and turned to see her profile. She winked her blue-gray eyes and made faces at herself, laughing at her silliness.

Autumn watched herself in the mirror as she towel-dried and braided her long auburn hair. Something was off, but she wasn't sure what. It was like when someone with a new haircut catches sight of themselves and is surprised by their own reflection. They see what they expect, but don't expect what they see. The nightmare must have hit her harder than she thought.

There was a knock at the bathroom door. "Your things are on the bed," Kali called through the locked door. "Breakfast is almost ready. Be quick, or your food will be cold before you've put your feet beneath the table."

"I'll be downstairs in a minute Auntie-ji."

"I've left some nice warm clothes on your bed for you. Dry your hair well, or you'll catch a chill."

"Yes Auntie-ji."

"And don't forget to put on your slippers."

"I won't Auntie-ji." Autumn listened for the closing of the bedroom door. *I can use a computer, but she still doesn't believe I know which end to put my underwear on. Put your underpants on your head once when you're two and you're branded for life.*

She opened the bathroom door. The bedroom dwarfed her double bed. The door to the hallway seemed miles away. The furniture seemed familiar. Had it been at the place she'd lived in before? Or maybe she was just remembering it wrong.

Some small shopping bags were on her dresser. Inside she found a new toothbrush and fresh toothpaste, a new hairbrush, and new deodorant. The second bag contained some mascara, a couple of palettes of eyeshadow, some eyeliner sticks, and a few tubes of lipstick, all still in their pretty silver boxes.

Autumn started to dress. She was tempted to go downstairs with her bra on her head, just to tease Kali. She tried it on, posing in her lace, B-cup hat. Someone was laughing. She grabbed her shirt and towel, covering her breasts. She searched the corners of the room. No one was there.

She slipped into the bathroom to finish dressing. Her hands shook as she buttoned her shirt. Nightmares and a strange bed in a strange room, that's all it was. She'd remember everything in a little while. That's what Kali had said. She remembered being Autumn Rose Cassidy, and if she could remember that she would always know who she was. Even if she wasn't quite sure where she was or what was going on around her.

Autumn took a deep breath and went back into her bedroom. The quiet was unnerving. She threw the packaging from her toothbrush, toothpaste, and makeup into a blue garbage can. A second can for waste stood beside it. She remembered a young girl standing in front of the dresser, reading a speech she had prepared for school. The two cans had been part of the presentation. The girl stood tall, index cards in her hands, a speech entitled "What We Can Do for the Environment."

Who was this little girl? How did Autumn know her?

Recycling. There was something important she had to remember, and it had to do with recycling.

Her ears started ringing. The noise condensed into words, into her name. She knew the voice from her nightmare. The corners of the room whispered to her. The clock radio flashed to life. Blood, Sweat, and Tears sang about a spinning wheel. The song from the car crash. The song from her nightmare.

Autumn hurried from the room. Maybe she'd sleep someplace else tonight.

***

*A*utumn reached for the last piece of toast in the basket. She slathered it with peanut butter and took a big bite. It was so good, that she almost hugged herself from sheer joy.

Kali put down her teacup and smiled. "Have you had enough to eat?"

Autumn stole the last piece of bacon from the plate as the butler cleared away the dishes. "Everything was just delicious. You'd think I'd never eaten before."

"We've traveled a long way. With all of the upset, you always wake up ready to eat an elephant or three. But everything will become normal again soon. Not to worry."

"Auntie-ji, I think there's something wrong with me. It might sound strange, but I don't remember where we were before. The other place you were talking about? I have no clue where that was."

"Well, what do you remember?"

"Before waking up in that bedroom this morning? Nothing. I don't even remember going to sleep in that room last night."

"What about earlier memories? Do you remember your parents?"

"I remember that I was born in India. I remember that the place was hot, but I don't remember much else about living there because I was about seven years old when we left. I remember growing up in Kent, England, and my father remarried there. I remember moving to Canada when my father was transferred here. I remember my step-mother was a real cow who left the country with my stepbrother as soon as my father's will was read. And I think I was only about twelve years old at the time?" Autumn reached for Kali's hand. "And I remember you, Auntie-ji, standing with me through all of my memo-ries." Autumn smiled and squeezed Kali's hand before reaching for her mug. "My magical godmother. Next to you, Cinderella's crew wouldn't even qualify to make a dog's dinner."

"Thank you, *Beti*. I think." She lay her spoon across the top of the cup. The butler nodded and removed Kali's dishes and cup. "*Beti*, you just need to rest."

"But what about my memory Auntie-ji? Am I going through some kind of emotional problem? Grief? Exhaustion? Was I on some kind of medication?"

"*Beti*, just give it time. You are so impatient."

"I lost my father, my stepmother, and my brother in a matter of what, months? And if I was ill as well…"

"Those would seem to be very good reasons for your short-term memory to not work well. But *Beti*…"

"Hopefully I won't wake up tomorrow forgetting about today," Autumn said, before taking a last bite of toast. The dining room was impressive. The table could seat twenty without difficulty. The door to the serving area of the kitchen was painted the same shade of burgundy as the surrounding walls. The tray the butler carried back to the kitchen held fine china.

The colors in the room seemed to come from a painting hanging over the buffet. It was a landscape of a lake in the fall. The golds and the reds covering the hills around the lake reminded her of something. A place she was happy. But there was something else. Something horrible.

The nightmare! The accident in the dream happened in those mountains.

"Auntie-ji, whose house is this?"

"Yours. This is your house."

"I'm sixteen. How could I afford a house like this?"

"Oh, well, that." Kali folded her napkin and put it on the table. "Things will become clearer soon." Kali must have noticed the look of disappointment on Autumn's face. She sighed.

"Most recently it belonged to Rose Sterling. She lived here with her husband, Edward."

Those were the same names as the people in her nightmare. "Were these people related to me? Were they my grandparents? Where are they now?"

"Your grandparents? I guess they were, in a way. They were killed in a car accident a short while ago. Now, *Beti*, let us speak of more immediate concerns."

"Auntie-ji! Are you saying I inherited this house from Rose Sterling? My grandmother? How could she have been my grandmother? I don't remember her at all."

"Rose's will names you as her granddaughter and her heir." Kali waved her hand dismissively. "The story told in the will was that Rose's first husband, who would have to have been your grandfather, stole your father away during a messy divorce. She never saw your father again. Rose only learned of your existence recently."

"After my father died?"

"She added an extra clause in her will leaving her property to her granddaughter and namesake Autumn Rose Cassidy," Kali said, as if by rote. "It will all become clear in a little while. Truly Autumn. You are concerning yourself with trivial matters."

Autumn looked at the table. Breakfast was threatening to make a reappearance. For ten seconds she had a real family. Not the Cinderella story she remembered. Trivial matters? A father who was ex-military and always traveling. A stepfamily who gave her the skills to be independent, so they could ship her off the first chance they got. They were her family at least until her father's death. When they found out they would have no control over the full Cassidy estate, they couldn't get themselves away fast enough.

But Rose had Eddie, which means she remarried. Kali might know if there were other family members. She might have an aunt or an uncle or both. Or maybe more than one of each. They might have kids. She could have cousins.

"Can we talk about Rose's life?"

"*Beti* we can talk more about this later. I think we have more important things to discuss now."

Autumn leaned across the table. "But Auntie-ji, I want to know more about Rose and her family. There's so much I need to know. I have so many questions."

Autumn noticed a change in the bone beads around Kali's neck. They had grown from the size of a thumbnail to the size of her hand. They weren't the abstract carvings Autumn thought they were either. Each bead was a skull. A miniature human skull. And they all seemed to be looking at her. Kali's warm gold skin seemed to be developing a cold steel-blue undertone. She looked into Kali's large dark eyes as the whites turned black. Kali's lipstick started to deepen from a subtle pink to a deep vampire red.

Autumn nodded. "But I can save that all for later." She pasted on a smile and wiped her sweating hands on the cloth napkin in her lap to hide their shaking. She tried to slow her breathing so breakfast didn't make a quick exit in the other direction. "We were going to talk about a project we're working on?"

Kali stood up. Everything from the beads to her lipstick returned to normal. She seemed to hear something and tilted her head to listen. "*Beti*, I have some work to attend to first. Have a look around the house. It might help you remember. Mind the blood on the floor. My skirt must have dripped."

They left the dining room. But by the time Autumn entered the hallway, Kali was already gone. Autumn walked up the hall and opened the door to a library. Maplewood shelves lined the walls, each filled with an impressive number of leather-bound books. The only open wall held a fieldstone fireplace flanked by two matching wing-back chairs angled to share an oversized ottoman.

There was a small niche in the wall, not visible from the door. Autumn peeked inside. On one wall stood a simple bookcase filled with well-worn paperbacks. The other wall held a tall chest of drawers and, on the back wall, a glass-fronted cabinet.

The tall glass cabinet contained some large folios, with some over-sized books on the bottommost shelf. Ancient-looking scrolls with ivory finials sat on a narrow shelf near the top. Three clay tablets incised with short, wedge-shaped lines painted in an Egyptian style rested at eye-level.

Autumn leaned close to the glass and studied the painting on the pale stone. There was a piece missing from one corner, but the colors were so bright it could have been painted that morning.

She had seen it before. She didn't know where or when, but she remembered it. She studied the marks on the tablet and sounded out a couple of words. "Wonderful," she muttered. "I can't remember where I was yesterday, but my New Kingdom Egyptian is still pretty good."

The tablet was part of the Egyptian Book of the Dead. The passage talked about the different parts of a person's soul. All the folios and books in the cabinet were about finding the afterlife and spirit work.

The last cabinet was made of a pine aged to a honey-gold. The drawers were graduated, the smallest on the top, the largest at the bottom. Autumn opened the largest drawer in the cabinet and lifted out a rosewood box with vine leaves carved around the sides. An engraved silver plaque was centered on the top: E.M.C.—Elizabeth Marie Cassidy. This box had belonged to her mother.

Autumn couldn't remember her mother's face, but she remembered her father's face when he caught her trying on her mother's necklaces. She'd been around eight and she had taken a tablecloth from the linen closet and tied it around her neck like a cloak. Autumn paraded around her room, greeting the invisible guests to her royal tea party. She turned toward the door. Her father was there, watching her. She'd expected him to be angry for taking the box from his room, but he just seemed sad.

It was the only time he'd sat down and talked to her about her mother. When he married Mrs. Cassidy (she refused to be addressed as anything else), the box disappeared. Autumn thought it had been stolen. Had it been in Kali's care these last four years?

Had it only been four years since her father had passed? It felt like several lifetimes ago.

"Autumn? Here you are."

"I'm sorry Auntie-ji. I just found this in the drawer." She lightly brushed the carvings on the box. "I thought my mother's jewelry was gone forever. I was afraid Mrs. Cassidy had stolen it."

"Oh, that horrible woman." Kali shuddered as if she had tasted something sour or spoiled. "Her death was without honor, her afterlife reflecting the life she lived."

"She died? When? What about her son? Is he okay?"

"Autumn, please. We have a lot to do if you are to begin your work." Autumn sat down on the sofa beneath the window and lifted the box into her lap. Kali sighed. "Your mother's jewelry box." She rolled her beads between her fingers. "Your father was an honorable man, and far more insightful than his second wife gave him credit for. After he amended his will, he gave me the box for safekeeping. It's to be entrusted to you again at the end of October, on the eve of your next birthday."

"Thank you Auntie-ji. For everything. For keeping it safe. For taking care of me."

"Enough sentimentality. It makes my sword-hand itchy. Come now. We have work to do." She sighed. "Please open the box."

Autumn lifted the lid and gently removed a gold heart set with rubies on a gold and garnet chain. "This was my mother's too. But everything else in the box..."

"These other pieces were bought for Rose, and by Rose. I had them placed in the jewelry box after the accident." Kali smiled as she admired a simple pendant with her image on it. "Your mother's family have always been able to see and speak to spirits. It was how she was able to call me." She replaced it in the box. "Rose worked with me for many years in Ville des Saintes. You will be doing as I taught you, taking over Rose's work, so I put her things with yours."

"My grandmother rescued ghosts? What about my mother? Was she working with you too?"

"No *Beti*. Just Rose."

"Is it a thing that skips a generation? Will my granddaughter replace me? Did Rose replace one of her grandparents?"

"Autumn, please. You ask so many questions... and all will be answered in good time. Now, can we get back to the discussion at hand?"

"Of course. I'm sorry." She found a silver cuff with small pieces of turquoise set to form a geometric flower. Autumn nodded at something Kali said. It was something historical. Autumn tried on the bracelet. She looked at Kali. There was a holy golden glow around her. Autumn looked at her own hand. The glow wasn't there.

She became a little lightheaded. Someone was moving around the room. She could see him from the corner of her eye. When she turned to look at him, he ducked into a shadow. Her heart beat a little bit faster.

*D*ance with me, Rosie.

"And this is the library," Rose said as she opened the door. It was almost Valentine's Day, 1967. Rose and Eddie were in their first year of graduate school. The sound of her clogs clattered across the hardwood floor. Kali had finally stopped giving her grief about her jeans, but the clogs were going to make Kali blue in the face —literally. She might even sprout an extra arm or three.

The tour hadn't progressed beyond the grounds and the first floor. Rose was convinced her godmother was standing guard on the stairs to the bedrooms. And Kali didn't need to wear her necklace of severed heads to intimidate Rose's boyfriends, not that she'd had the time or inclination for a relationship. Not before meeting Edward Marcus Sterling. Even his name sounded magical.

Eddie looked at some of the leather-bound books on the shelves. "Any of these first editions?"

"Some."

"This room is amazing." Eddie whistled as he looked at the woodwork and the plaster ceiling medallions. "I honestly don't know where to look first." The painting over the fireplace caught his eye. "Is that a Monet? An honest-to-goodness Monet?"

Rose nodded. He turned to study her face. He pointed over his shoulder with his thumb. "Monet?"

"Yes. And there's a Degas in the bedroom."

Eddie gasped. "Miss Rose! Are you inviting me into your bedroom to see your oil paintings?" He wiggled his eyebrows, and she laughed.

"If I need to pull something that obvious, I must be slipping." She put her arms around his waist. "It would, however, get us past my guardian."

He bent down and kissed her on the nose. "The wonder of it all is I thought I was marrying you for love. Now it turns out I can marry you for your money too." He looked over his shoulder. "It's a real, live, honest-to-goodness Monet."

Rose held his face between her hands, turning him back to face her. "Yes."

"Yes? Yes what?"

"Yes, you silly man. I will marry you." And she kissed him.

Autumn struggled to pull off the cuff. "Auntie-ji, what just happened?" Her heartbeat felt like she had run a marathon.

"Nothing happened, except you weren't listening to a word I said. You put on the bracelet, studied the bracelet's workmanship, and then took it off." Kali put the cuff back into the box. "I should warn you, all of the pieces in here, from the small diamond earrings to the big platinum moon pendant, have been charmed to help you see ghosts and to help the ghosts relay messages to you. And that includes the bracelet."

"What does it mean?"

"We have discussed this before. Don't you remember?"

What Autumn wanted to scream was, "No Auntie-ji. I don't remember. I don't remember anything. Not where we lived before we came here. Not the name of the last book I read. Not even what we ate for dinner last night."

But what she did say was, "I guess it was seeing my mother's ruby pendant, which I thought my stepmother stole. And seeing my grandmother's jewelry. I never knew her, so I guess the only way I'll ever learn anything about her is through her things, like this house or that bracelet."

"I think I understand." Kali nodded. "You have yet to regain your memory, and there are many things to come to terms with." Autumn stopped looking at the box and met Kali's eyes. Kali continued. "Do you remember what to do when you encounter a ghost in need of assistance?"

Autumn nodded. "Dealing with a ghost—explain to them they are dead, either by introducing them to the current reality or by pretending I'm a part of the life they remember and are reliving. Then I help them find their relatives to take them to the afterlife."

There was a tool… someplace. She looked inside the rosewood box and pulled out a small egg-shaped crystal. It was clear, but it changed from light blue to deep purple depending on how the light hit it.

"You found it. Do you remember this stone, *Beti?*"

"Just that it has something to do with ghosts."

"This stone will make the spirit more easily visible to you and help them acknowledge you through their delusion. It will also help you send them on their way, but only if they're willing."

"Where did the stone come from?"

"It was a gift from The Moirai—the Three Fates. The stone allows the ghosts to become untangled from the tapestry of time. It makes the Fates' work easier when the souls of the dead don't stay woven into the affairs of the living."

Autumn was going to ask why but thought better of it. She thought about the person watching her from the corners of her room. Maybe she would bring the box upstairs, have a little heart-to-heart, and see if there was a way to get rid of the Peeping Tom. Or at least set some ground rules about when he could come to hang out.

Kali stood up. "Today you get used to your surroundings again. Get your bearings. Tomorrow we start work."

"Where will I start?"

Kali looked over at the mantle and seemed to track some movement. Her eyes narrowed. "Seems we won't have to look far at all."

Autumn became a bit worried for her new friend. If he was tied to the house in some way, he might have some of the answers about her grandmother's life. "Auntie-ji, um, he seems harmless. Can he stick around, please? For practice?"

Kali seemed a bit puzzled. "Yes, you may keep him. For now."

"Mom, I'm home!" Zoe yelled as she kicked off her sneakers and slid her backpack across the floor. It landed with a thunk against the leg of the hall table.

"I'm in the kitchen," Nora called.

Zoe handed her mother the mail. "Pierre, at the desk, said it was late today. He signed for a registered letter." She stole a piece of carrot from the cutting board. "It's the one on the top."

Nora wiped her hands on a towel and pushed her graying black hair behind her ear. "Your laundry is on your bed. Please try to get it into the drawers this time. And the application to De Sousa Junior College is on your desk." Nora had Rose's features, but her father's black Irish coloring. "How's your portfolio coming?" She took the letters and the store flyers to the breakfast table at the bay window. It separated the dining room from the spacious living room.

Zoe sat opposite Nora. "It's coming. I'll have everything ready for the March deadline." She opened the newspaper to the comics section. The natural light coming through the window began to fade. Nora opened the small café lamp in the center of the round table. The lamp's reflection mixed with the cityscape. Ella Fitzgerald's voice made its way into the room from the player in the kitchen. The colors of Snowy Hill took a final bow in the setting sun.

"So, does the lawyer say when we can move into the museum? I mean Rowan House." Zoe glanced at her mother before answering a text.

Nora continued reading the letter from her parents' lawyer. Zoe looked up at her mother's sigh. Nora held the letter as if she and her hand were no longer speaking. She stared out the window, expressionless. "Mom?"

"Things are going to be a little more complicated than I thought."

"So, you and Dad are going to court? Again?" The battle was an old one, and she couldn't keep the exasperation out of her voice.

"There's something I need to talk to you about." Nora ran her nail against the fold in the letter. "Can you put your phone away for a minute, please?"

Zoe put her phone on the table, screen down, ignoring the chime from the reply to her last text.

Nora took a deep breath. "Grandpa Eddie wasn't Grandmother Rose's first husband. She was married before. Her ex-husband got custody of their son, who has since died." She picked up the letter again. "My mother's estate, including Rowan House, has been inherited by her granddaughter and namesake Autumn Rose Cassidy."

"And she didn't even tell you about him?"

"She did. She told my father and me about them after my brother was gone."

"Mom I'm so sorry." Zoe took her mother's hand. "How are you still so calm?"

"What am I supposed to do?" Nora tried to smile. She failed miserably. "I had a brother. I had a brother named James Cassidy. I never knew what he looked like. I never knew where he lived. I never knew how he died. I wish I'd learned more about him. I wish they had let me meet him. I wish we had been able to be real siblings. But that's all gone. There's nothing more to it."

"I think I'd feel better if you yelled or threw something."

"Sorry to disappoint you, honey. I'm afraid that's something my mother did leave me. Stoic in the face of adversity."

"It's all so strange. Why wasn't I told? What happened to 'tell it like it is'?"

"I don't know honey. We were planning to tell you everything. Your cousin was supposed to come to the anniversary party. My dad was trying to set things up as a surprise for your grandmother. But…" She waved her hands as if to pull her feelings and words from the air.

"So that's it? This new granddaughter, Autumn Rose, is just going to get everything? Grandpa Eddie's painting hanging in the dining room? The cart in the living room where Grandma Rose and I held our tea parties? The chairs in the library where they helped me learn to read? Everything?"

"Honey, I'm sorry. But there's more."

"How is that fair? They were my grandparents—not hers! I knew them. I loved them." Zoe could feel her fingernails cutting into her palm. "She's nobody! How can this happen?"

"Honey, I need you to listen for another minute."

Tears gathered in Zoe's eyes, but she was too angry to let them fall. "She's taken everything. She's ruined everything. I hate her!"

Zoe stormed out of the room. Nora called after her, but Zoe ignored her. She slammed her bedroom door, put her headphones on, and cranked the volume until she thought her ears would bleed. Only when she was sure she wouldn't be able to hear herself, did she begin to sob.

*It* was well after seven when Zoe knocked on Nora's bedroom door. "I'm sorry Mom. I didn't mean to be such a brat." Zoe had thought her eyes were swollen, but her mother's mascara striped her cheek, and her eyes looked like she'd been on the wrong side of a prize fight. Zoe hated to see her mother cry.

Nora sat up and patted the settee beside her, lifting the afghan so Zoe could snuggle up with her under a knitted blanket in shades of blue, red, and purple. Rose had taught Zoe to knit when she was eleven. Together, they knit all the blanket's squares and created the afghan for Nora's fortieth birthday. It used to feel like a hug from Rose, but today it just felt like a blanket.

Nora kissed her daughter's cheek. "Do you want something to eat?" Her voice seemed a bit hoarse.

"How about we order a pizza?" Her mother's favorite comfort food.

"Sounds like a plan." Neither of them moved. Nora put her arm around Zoe as their heads leaned in together.

Zoe wanted to leave everything alone, to forget about cousins, and houses, and inheritances, and... "Mom? What are we going to do about her? Autumn Rose, I mean."

"That's what I wanted to talk to you about. The will said Autumn's father appointed Rose as legal guardian. But Rose made my father the executor of her estate. Eddie would be responsible for part of Autumn's upbringing and her finances."

"So?"

"When Grandma Rose put that clause into her will, Grandpa Eddie added a codicil to his. His wishes were I take over the role of executor, which includes raising Autumn."

"Is she going to move in here? I'm not sharing my room."

"Hold it. Please stop and listen for two minutes. I swear. You are so impatient."

Nora put her arm around Zoe's shoulder again. "My father worked very hard to find Mom's son. There had been some letters from private investigators and some false leads, but Grandpa never was able to find him. Rose was heartbroken when she found out he had died."

"But what about *her*? What if this other Autumn Rose is a fake? What if she tricked Grandma Rose, telling her she's her granddaughter when she isn't even related to us? People do that, you know. Feed old people a plate full of drama, so they can scam them out of their money. There are scam warnings on FriendlyFaces all the time."

"Or we could arrange to meet her. We could invite her to dinner here and find out more about her."

"Here? What if she's a con artist? What if she comes here and murders us for Grandpa Eddie's money, so she can have everything?"

"Overreacting much?" Nora raised Zoe's chin, so she could look into her eyes. "Your grandfather was nobody's fool. He made sure every line was straight, and every angle was at ninety degrees before he accepted the other guardian's assurances Autumn Rose was her granddaughter."

Zoe nodded. "So, what do we do?"

"We have to contact her and her guardian so we can figure everything out. That's my legal responsibility. But we have a choice: to welcome her as a member of the family, or I can deal with everything on my own until she comes of age. At which point she gets on with her life, and we get on with ours."

She hugged Zoe. "We might be the only family Autumn has left. My mother said James was a widower. It means Autumn lost her mother while he was still alive, when Rose wrote the will. Her father is gone, and now, so is Rose."

"Why should we even care? She's got a big house and all of Rose's money. She'll have tons of friends in no time. For all we know, she's having a party every night. Inviting all kinds of hipsters and weird people to ruin that fine historic house."

"Zoe, isn't that the same place you keep calling *the museum*?"

"Mom!"

"Zoe?"

"Can't we go back to being just us? Can we just forget all about this Autumn Rose and her drama?"

"We can't. No, *you* can. I have a legal responsibility." Nora adjusted the blanket. "And I'm curious about her. We don't know anything about her or her father." Nora got that faraway look in her eye which meant she was making a decision Zoe was probably not going to like. "Zoe, I think we both should meet her, at least once. Whether we agree with Rose's decision or not, she's still our family. We might be all she has left."

"That's not our fault!"

"Zoe, please. She's all alone in that big house."

"If she's even there," Zoe said. "I mean, we know she inherited the house, but not if she's living in it or anything. We don't even know if she's in Ville des Saintes, let alone in Canada."

"True. The letter never said where she lived. Maybe we should try calling the lawyer." She looked over at the clock on the bedside table. "I guess it will have to wait for tomorrow."

"Unless we try the house and see if anyone answers the phone." As soon as the words left her lips, Zoe wished people came with a *delete* button.

"Good point." Nora pushed the blanket aside and patted Zoe's knee. "Let's get up, wash our faces, and..."

"Order pizza?"

"First we'll call for pizza, and then call the house and see if Uncle Theo is there, and if he knows about Autumn Rose."

Zoe nodded and folded up the blanket while Nora went into the kitchen to find the takeout menu. Zoe was lost in thought. On the one hand, she hated being caught in a conundrum (Taylor's old word of the week). And she did want all the facts about this mysterious new relative. On the other hand, she wanted to go back to before the letter. She wanted to go back to the time before cousins, and wills, and graveyard projects. She wanted to go back to when she was just a girl missing her grandparents.

Nora called to her from the other room. "Pepperoni or sausage?"

"Let's go nuts." Zoe placed the blanket at the end of the settee. "Get both."

Zoe paced from one end of the sofa to the other. Nora was on the phone with Kali Shyama, Autumn's guardian. The pleasantries were over. It seems Kali was not one for small talk. They had moved on to the subject of the *other* granddaughter.

"So, Autumn Rose is living in Rowan House now? How is she settling in?"

Zoe stopped. She remembered what the twins had said about drugs and wild parties. "How old is she?" she whispered.

Nora asked the question. "So, she and Zoe are the same age?" Nora doodled on the notepad by the phone. "She and my mother shared a birthday? How odd."

At least Zoe knew she was a few months older than her cousin. Older, wiser, senior—Zoe was the first edition granddaughter.

Nora laid the pen on the pad. "I think it's time for us to meet."

Zoe started pacing again. She didn't like the look in her mother's eyes. She opened her mouth to ask a question, but Nora held her hand up to silence her.

"The girl is *my niece* after all. Yes, I realize that Kali. True, but it was clearly spelled out in the lawyer's letter. She's only sixteen, for Heaven's sake. And I'm her nearest blood relative." Nora took a deep breath. "And according to my parents' wills, she is my responsibility. I should have some say in her care."

Zoe's eyes went wide. "You want to bring her here? To live?"

Nora sighed. "Of course. I realize all of that. That's not what I'm saying. I'm sure my mother trusted you, if it was her son's wish. It's a non-issue. But think of the girl. This whole episode must have come as quite a shock to her. She's spent her whole life thinking she was alone in the world, only to discover that she had a secret family she knew nothing about." There was a slight catch in her voice. Zoe took her hand.

Nora nodded and smiled slightly. "I think Autumn Rose would benefit from meeting us. Knowing we are more than just names in a lawyer's letter."

Nora looked shocked "Not a word about us?" She shook her head. "Mature or not—she's still only sixteen! What you're proposing is too much for her to carry. And it's all the more reason for us to meet. She should learn about us, about her family. She has to know she's not alone in the world."

Kali must have said the wrong thing. The look on Nora's face was usually reserved for those who were about to be grounded.

"What's she saying?" Zoe whispered.

Nora held up her index finger. "You are her guardian, according to James's will, but I'm a blood relation and also my parents' executor." She rolled her eyes. "It says so in Rose's and Edward's wills."

Zoe sat down in the chair opposite her mother and waited silently, chewing the inside of her cheek.

Nora's face became flushed. "Her father was my older half brother." She pressed her lips together and inhaled sharply. "Fine. Let's do it your way. I'll start by contacting child protective services, and I have a friend in Family Court who'll tell me what my rights are and what I have to do to get full custody of my niece. And then..." Nora waited. "Only dinner, so we can meet. Just to let her know she has a family. Please have Thanatos bring her by on Friday, at around 6:30. Good night, Madam Kali, and thank you." Nora hung up the phone.

Zoe interlaced her fingers. "So she's coming here?"

"Just for dinner baby." Nora took her purse from the hook in the coat closet, slipped a nitroglycerin tablet under her tongue, and put the pizza money on the entry table.

Zoe had noticed her mother taking her heart medicine. Time to get everything Zen again. When she stood beside her mom and hugged her, she noticed how tired Nora looked. "We'll find out everything there is to find out about this Autumn Rose. There won't be any more secrets."

"But there will be pizza." Nora smiled and kissed Zoe on the cheek. "Lots and lots of pizza."

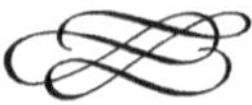

*A*utumn lay in bed with her eyes closed. The alarm went off as set at 8:30 a.m. The radio host took calls from listeners participating in some kind of trivia contest. Autumn listened, telling herself she needed to keep her eyes closed so she could concentrate, seeing if she could remember any of the answers to the questions.

The truth was, she was afraid to open her eyes. She'd been afraid every day. Sure, she remembered being in this bed and in this house yesterday. But that didn't mean anything. She'd opened them the other morning, and the world went wrong. What if she opened her eyes, and everything was different again? What if everything she thought she'd done yesterday happened last week, or last month, or, Heaven forbid, last year? What if she were waking up in a different house in a different city?

What if she opened her eyes, and didn't recognize anyone? Or worse, no one knew who she was.

There was a knock at the door. "Autumn?" Kali said. "I have your tea. It's time to get out of bed and start your day."

Kali was at the door. And she had her tea. Just like yesterday. Just like every morning this week. Autumn opened her eyes and sat up. It was still the same room. She threw off the covers. She wore the same pajamas she remembered putting on last night. The commercial ended, and she stiffened. The radio announcer said he was going to play a Beatles song in honor of Throwback Thursday. Yesterday had been Wednesday.

"Coming Auntie-ji." She did a little happy dance to *Twist and Shout.* Autumn opened her bedroom door.

"Why was your door locked, *Beti?*" Kali asked.

"I don't remember locking it." Autumn noticed the key. It hadn't been there when she'd gone to bed.

Kali scanned the room. Her eyes narrowed, and the skulls on her necklace began to gnash their teeth. "Not to worry about silly things." Kali's smile didn't reach her eyes. Her skin had lost its friendly glow. "This is an old home, with old inconsequential bits and old contrary pieces." She seemed to be talking to the corner beside the dresser. "But I have experience with bothersome things. I know how to make them disappear when they don't behave. It's always best for everyone's spirit when these things cooperate, so we can all get along."

Autumn wasn't sure how the key or the dresser felt, but she was relieved she was talking to them and not to her. She thanked Kali for the tea and went to sit at the edge of the bed.

"Kali? Do I go to school, or do I study with a tutor here at the house?"

"I don't understand the question."

"It's just that it's October, and school begins in September. Am I registered for high school someplace?"

Kali sat on the bed beside Autumn. "Do you want to go to school *Beti?* If you do, I can put it into my plans for today. But yesterday was an important day. I had the telephone conversation we have been waiting for."

"Is everything okay?"

"Yes, yes. Of course. Are *you* all right?" Kali seemed worried.

"It's probably nothing. It's just I'm still having trouble with my memory."

"The memories should be back soon. Nothing to be bothered

with." Kali took Autumn's free hand. "I told you about Rose, and her life, and her husband named Eddie."

Eddie. Autumn's stomach flipped. "And where is Eddie now?"

"He was in the car accident too. He didn't survive."

The tea tasted like leather on her tongue. All Autumn could do was nod.

Kali smiled. "Rose and Eddie had a daughter named Nora."

Autumn paused for a moment. "And she's dead too."

"What a horrible thing to say! Of course she's not dead. How can you think something like that?" Kali calmed herself. "Nora lives in Ville des Saintes. She's divorced. Nora has a daughter, Zoe, who's sixteen. So, she's about your age now."

"I have an aunt? And a cousin? A family? A real blood family?" Autumn stopped. "Oh, Auntie-ji, you know I love you and Uncle Theo with my whole heart, but it's just... They're like me. You know, mortal. Human. You and Uncle Theo are immortal. They'll know what it feels like for life to be finite. You understand, right?"

"I believe I understand *Beti*, and you will understand more when your memory returns." She patted Autumn's hand. "There's more to tell. Your *new aunt* was named in the will as an executor of Rose's estate, and she will be acting as your guardian too. Although I tried to dissuade her, you have been invited to dinner at her home on Friday night."

"Dinner? Friday? What will I wear? What should I bring? What should I do?"

"I suggest you go to the mall. You can find yourself something nice to wear to meet your family. You can find a gift for your hostess. And you can begin your work for me."

utumn waited outside by the door. Thanatos was bringing the car around. When she'd put on the necklace with Kali's image on it, she saw the golden glow around him. He was another of the Agents of Death she would be working with. Had she seen the glow before?

She watched the sparse traffic pass the estate's front gate. She couldn't remember the last time she'd been outside and wasn't sure if she remembered what the city looked like. Was it a trick of her funky memory, or was it just because there had been a lot going on? She'd had her lessons with Kali about helping ghosts and lost souls. They opened several rooms that apparently hadn't seen the light of day in years. And then there were all the clothes she'd found in the spare room. All of the boxes with her name on them. She just couldn't remember herself as being so... bohemian.

The clothes were authentic, all dating back to the 1960s and early 1970s. It all looked like something you'd expect to find at a love-in or the original Woodstock: bell-bottom jeans and gauzy blouses made from Indian cotton. Some skirts were very short; others went down to her ankles. Some had designer labels, some had labels from stores long gone. She must have spent hours and hours on the internet and running around the city, rummaging through vintage shops and garage sales, looking for the perfect pieces, investing most of her spare time and cash into this extensive wardrobe. How could she have forgotten all that time on the hunt?

Was that the type of thing she wore before she came to Ville des Saintes? Did her friends wear the same type of things? Where were her friends?

Autumn heard a sound coming from above, a joyous sound making her think of faraway places. She scanned the sky. There it was. The telltale 'V'. The Canadian geese flew above the house. The sound made her happy and sad at the same time. There used to be someone to share this with.

She closed her eyes to make a wish. Yes, it was silly and childish, but it couldn't hurt. She took a deep breath and wished she could remember her life—for better or for worse. She wanted her memory back.

"Sending your wish with the geese?" Uncle Theo stood beside her.

"Bravo *Koukla*. The geese seem to be in a good mood. They'll carry the wish to those who look after those things."

"Do you believe in that too?"

"I don't know. But they are always an omen of change. Maybe your wish will make things change in your favor."

*hanatos merged the gray Audi into the traffic around Snowy Hill, which headed to the downtown core. At a light, a sleek car with huge tail-light fins stopped ahead of them. Autumn thought she would look great in a car like that, especially wearing the clothes she'd found in the boxes. She'd be behind the wheel, watching the sun come up over the city after a big party at one of the converted lofts in the Rag District. She'd blush when the milkman winked knowingly as she passed him on the front step. She'd tiptoe in, milk bottles in her hand, platform shoes sticking out of her purse, hoping not to wake anyone in the house. But Kali would be at the kitchen table, waiting. When they say death never sleeps—it's true. There was no sneaking past that woman and her grinning necklace.

But Autumn couldn't drive a car, let alone a classic convertible like the one pulling away from the light. She didn't even have a driver's license. Did she even know anyone in the Rag District, and if she did, why hadn't they called her?

The car signaled to turn left. The driver was an older man with gray hair. Had he waved at them, or just at the driver who'd let him by? A shiver went up her spine. A memory? A memory of something she'd heard?

Thanatos turned on the radio and put on a community station. The announcer talked about hockey, switching seamlessly between Greek, English, and French.

Autumn let her mind drift. What was her family going to be like? Would they be as nervous to meet her as she was to meet them? Would she look like them? Would they love her?

*I*f Autumn hadn't been confused before, Temple Mall would have set the stage and played the opening number. Despite it being the beginning of October, some of the shops already had Christmas decorations in their windows. Right next door to a window full of sleighs and animated reindeer, a blow-up jack-o'-lantern was the focal point of a floor display. They passed a costume shop with a mannequin dressed in a Santa suit holding a chainsaw in one hand and a severed elf's head in the other. His jolly white beard stuck out of his hockey mask.

"Check this Eva. That's going to cost someone lots of money in therapy," said a man behind Autumn.

"For who Billy?" Eva said with a smile. "The kids who pass by this shop, or the person who dreamed that thing up?"

"Yes."

They laughed as they passed behind Autumn. Eva slipped her arm around Billy's waist. He kissed the top of her head.

Autumn noticed something odd. The couple was being followed by a second Eva. The copy didn't look like any ghost Autumn could remember. She looked like a faded black-and-white photo outlined in silver.

Autumn turned and gestured toward the couple. "Uncle Theo, what's going on? How is she being followed by her ghost?"

Thanatos looked around to see what Autumn was talking about. "No, *Koukla*. That's the woman's *Ka*. It's part of her soul. She must be very worried for her *Ka* to seem so faded. It should have more sparkle."

Autumn remembered a passage from the Book of the Dead she had found in the library. The *Ka* was the soul's messenger. It traveled from a person's body to the Higher Self, bringing emotional wisdom from this human plane of existence to where Universal Wisdom lived. And it brought inspiration and intuition from the Higher Self to the person here on Earth.

"Uncle, was I able to see *Ka* before?"

"I think so."

Before she could say another word, from out of nowhere Billy's *Ka* skateboarded down the thoroughfare, passing through people, benches, and kiosks without slowing.

The couple stopped. Autumn pretended to be interested in a window displaying small appliances as she watched them out of the corner of her eye.

Billy coughed into his elbow. Eva forced him to a stop. "Billy?" He didn't look well. There were bags under his eyes, and his shirt and pants were too big on him, and not in a stylish way.

"Eva, it was just a cough. Please don't make a big deal of it."

Eva's *Ka* looked on in despair. With each turn and trick, Billy's *Ka* became more solid and gained more color. What would happen when the *Ka* became identical to the host? Could it wander away and become lost? What would happen to the living Billy? Would Eva's *Ka* chase after it and become lost too? Would they both die?

Theo nodded. "That's why her *Ka* is so worried. He's been sick, and his *Ka* became separated from his host. He won't be able to heal completely if it doesn't come back into place properly."

Autumn watched as Eva's *Ka* started to become more desperate. "Is there something I can do?"

"Give me the ghost stone please," Thanatos said. Autumn handed it to him. He closed his fist over it. When he handed it back, the stone seemed to be sweating. The residue was oily and smelled like summer rain. "The ghost stone will help a *Ka* that has to leave the body. If it's stuck, a little of the oil on the person's skin will release the *Ka*. Then the person will feel like they are inspired to finish projects or do things to leave this world without regrets."

"Sort of like ghost prevention?"

"I like that."

"But what about them? Billy's *Ka* needs to be put back where it belongs, not let go."

Thanatos took a second stone out of his pocket. It was the same size and shape as the ghost stone, except it was black with a silver sheen inside it. "Let's call this one the Earth stone. The oil it gives will help reattach the *Ka* to the host. It will make sure the person gets well, physically, emotionally, and spiritually."

The oil from the Earth stone felt grittier on Autumn's fingers, and it smelled like fresh-cut grass. Autumn weighed the stones in her hands. "How will I know which to use when I see an unhealthy *Ka?*"

Thanatos thought for a moment. He asked to see the pendant with Kali's image on it. Autumn took it from beneath her shirt. Thanatos touched it and said something in Greek. "Look at the couple again."

Kali's image hovered at Billy's shoulder. But it wasn't Auntie-ji— it was Kali with her swords and severed heads. Considering the Goddess's size, she sort of looked like a Barbie doll the demented Santa from that shop window would have left for some unsuspecting child.

"If you see Kali at the person's shoulder, touch their skin with the oil from the black stone to bring them back to themselves. If you see Kali beside the person's legs, use the ghost stone's oil, to let them go."

Autumn nodded as she studied the stones. When she looked up, Thanatos had disappeared. Time to jump in with both feet. Autumn adjusted the shoulder strap of her purse and trailed after the couple.

Autumn watched them continue on, then followed. She tried to keep the theme from *Mission: Impossible* from running through her head. It didn't work. She ducked behind a clothing rack and pretended to tie her shoe.

Neither Eva nor Billy acted as if there was a problem. But Eva's *Ka* knew. The *Ka* walked back and forth across the aisle, sometimes hanging back, and putting her hands to her mouth, soundlessly calling out. She looked so sad and forlorn. Billy's *Ka* hadn't a care in the world. He jumped his skateboard over benches and down handi-capped ramps.

Autumn wiped her sweating palms on the legs of her jeans. The couple had stopped in front of a pet store. A mechanical dog wagged its tail and sat down beside a doll dressed for trick-or-treating. Eva put her arms around Billy, and he held her close. Her *Ka* wept.

Autumn strolled over to the window and bent to look at the cat toys and aquarium supplies. She wasn't sure if her anxiety was caused by this new experiment, or if the crappy mall music was getting on her nerves. Kali's image was still above Billy's shoulder: reattach the *Ka*.

She put her hand in the pocket of her leather jacket and held the black stone tightly. The couple was moving away.

Eva glanced at the window of a jewelry store. Billy stopped short. His face was calm as he looked in the window. Eva laughed and tried to pull him onward. He didn't move toward the entrance of the store but didn't keep walking either. His *Ka* rode in a circle around them, eventually kicking the board into his hand. The *Ka* seemed to be saying something to Billy, but Billy didn't react or seem to understand. The *Ka* shrugged and got back on the skateboard. Billy wasn't getting inspiration from his *Ka* anymore either. Autumn had to act.

She rubbed the stone against the back of her hand and casually strolled up beside the couple. Autumn opened her purse and pretended to search for something, as she *accidentally* brushed the back of Billy's hand.

Her arm felt warm like it would on a sunny spring day. Billy's *Ka* stopped tooling around. The skateboard vanished into the shadows.

Autumn chewed on her lip, hoping this was what was supposed to happen. Billy's *Ka* raised its arms above its head like it was stretching after a long nap. The *Ka*'s color began to normalize to black and white, and the silver color returned to match Eva's. The *Ka* looked around as if it were trying to figure out where it was. It saw Billy and fell into step. The couple turned to leave, but Billy's *Ka* stopped him, looked him straight in the eye, and said something. Both Billys smirked.

Billy whispered something into Eva's ear. He stood tall and grinned. "Trick or treat?"

Eva's *Ka* jumped into Billy's *Ka*'s waiting arms, wrapped her legs around his waist, and covered his face with kisses. Seeing Billy's *Ka* back home was all the medicine Eva's *Ka* needed, and it quickly returned to normal.

"Well?" Billy put his arms around Eva.

She laughed. "It took you long enough." Eva wrapped her arms around Billy's neck and kissed him passionately. They walked, hand-in-hand, into the jewelry store.

Autumn wanted to jump into the air and shout out to the world.

"Well done, *Koukla*." Thanatos sat on a bench between two potted plants, a store-flyer on his knee.

"It was amazing, except..." She reached into her pocket. It was perfectly dry. She pulled out the stone. It was as clean as when Thanatos had given it to her.

"Don't worry about your clothes," Thanatos said. "The mixture will come to the outside of the stone when it needs to, and it leaves everything clean when you're done."

"Excellent." She clapped her hands. "One *Ka* rescued. No ghosts on this side of the mall. Our work is done. Let's go home."

Thanatos shook his head. "Sorry, *Koukla mou*. We are here until the stores close."

"That's at least another four hours." Autumn hoped it didn't sound as whiny to Uncle Theo as it did to her own ears.

"How about we go have some coffee? You'll look for ghosts. You'll watch the living. Study their *Ka*. See what they do and learn things about what you see."

Autumn agreed. Thanatos offered his arm, and they went to find the food court.

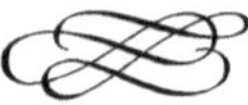

*A*utumn sipped her coffee, waiting for Thanatos to speak. Nothing. She sighed. "Do you have any words of wisdom about the *Ka*? Anything I should know, or look for, or work on?"

He blew across the top of his cup. "Nope." He took a drink.

The two elderly women who'd been sitting at the next table got up to leave. Thanatos smiled and nodded. One of the women smiled back and wished them both a wonderful day. The other woman looked a bit uncomfortable.

Autumn looked for the first woman's *Ka*. It wasn't there. Autumn opened her mouth to speak, but Thanatos said, "She's going to have a stroke. A week from Thursday. Her *Ka* has been very busy. Nothing to worry about, *Koukla*."

Autumn watched the women walk away, sharing a laugh. Her story would be over in a little over a week. It might even be the last time they see each other. Her friend would have this day's memories to carry with her for the rest of her life. And that's all she would be after that fateful Thursday. A memory.

Someone shouted, "Hey! Guys! Table!"

Three teenage boys rushed to sit down. One jogged behind Thanatos, knocking his back with his backpack, and spilling some of

Thanatos's coffee on his hands. Thanatos turned and watched the green-haired boy sit cross-legged in the middle of the table.

"Yeah?" The boy smirked. "Whatcha want? Some of this?" He grabbed his crotch. His friends started laughing.

Thanatos turned back to Autumn. "*Koukla*, there are no secrets. To understand this work, you have to appreciate..."

The teens started laughing loudly. Autumn couldn't help but overhear their conversation. Kali and her father might have been strict with her upbringing, or maybe she just had a bit of a prudish nature, but Autumn had never heard so many swear words strung together into one sentence. Maybe it wouldn't have been so noticeable if they weren't so loud.

Thanatos seemed to take it all in stride. He turned to look at the green-haired teen.

"What are you looking at old man?" He pulled himself to the end of the table and bent to look Thanatos in the face. His friends laughed and patted him on the back.

"Me? Nothing." Thanatos let a smile creep across his face. "I'm looking at absolutely nothing." He continued to smile at the boy.

Autumn felt the energy in the space change and go silent; like it did during a blackout. Thanatos kept smiling at the boy, not breaking eye contact. The boy stopped smiling, he stopped talking. He shook off his friends' hands. They too became quiet.

The boy turned away from Thanatos, got off the table, and sat in one of the chairs, sitting furthest from Autumn's table. He wasn't looking at their table anymore, but his neck and back stiffened as if he fought the urge to turn around. He peeked over at them and met Thanatos's gaze. The boy's chin began to quiver.

His friend put his arm around the green-haired boy's shoulder. "The movie's going to start soon. Let's go." He looked into his friend's face. "Dude, come on. The movie is supposed to be epic. Let's go."

The boy with green hair nodded and stood up. His friends turned to leave. He came over to the table. "I'm sorry if we disturbed you, sir, miss. Have a good afternoon."

Thanatos nodded and turned back to his coffee. As the boy followed his friends, he pulled out his phone.

"Hello, Mom? Everything's fine. I just wanted to hear your voice and tell you I love you." He paused. "No, I'm not high." He laughed lightly and asked about her day.

Autumn looked at Thanatos. "Uncle Theo, that was a bit mean."

Thanatos shrugged. "I can always forgive a brush with death. But don't make him spill his coffee."

*Taylor* was mid-sentence when Zoe yanked her by the arm. They were hidden behind a potted fern strung with fairy lights, opposite the food court. The mall was crowded with shoppers looking for boots, winter wear, and Halloween decorations and costumes.

Taylor tried to move, but Zoe pulled her back behind the plant. "What are we doing?" Taylor asked.

"Over there," she whispered. "Uncle Theo is sitting with a strange girl."

"And?"

"Don't you get it? It has to be her!"

Taylor tried to peek above the concrete planter.

"Don't!" Zoe whispered harshly. "She'll see us!"

"But she doesn't know who we are." Taylor rolled her eyes at Zoe's confused expression. "And you're supposed to be the smart one." She sighed. "Do you think your cousin knows what you look like? Does she even know your name?"

"Probably not."

"Do you think your cousin's wandering the mall, looking for you?"

Zoe shook her head.

"So why are we hiding?" Taylor stepped out from behind the planter.

"I don't know. And please stop calling her my *cousin*. Using all those mental air quotes and italics is giving me a headache."

"So, what do we call her?"

"Her name is Autumn. Or we could call her *the bitch who stole my mother's inheritance,* but it's a bit long."

"Agreed. We'd forget what we wanted to say by the time we got it out. An acronym would be just as bad."

Zoe nodded. "And we already know too many people we've labeled *the bitch.*" She sighed. "Autumn it is."

"What do you think she's doing here? Besides spending your grandmother's money."

"Basically, spending my grandmother's money."

"Do you want to go over and say hello or something?"

"No. We came here because the new *Polka-Dot Death-Shroud* CD is being released today, and the band is here to perform and sign copies. Let's go."

"But you said you wanted to talk to your Uncle Theo about your grandparents. He's sitting right there."

Zoe looked over at their table. Autumn's back was to them. She wore an old leather jacket. Her auburn hair was the same color as Zoe's, tied in a braid with the end over her shoulder, just like Zoe's. And they were almost the same age.

Zoe imagined how Autumn must be feeling about all this; thinking, *This is it. I'm alone in the world,* only to find out she has a secret family. And the only reason she found out about this secret family was her grandmother, the one who could explain everything and answer all her questions, the person responsible for this whole tower of secrets, died. Zoe understood that part. Rose had pulled that trick on both of her granddaughters.

Maybe Taylor was right. They could go over and introduce themselves and... Autumn stood up. She wore Grandma Rose's moon pendant. The one Grandpa Eddie bought for Rose on their honeymoon.

Zoe's favorite. To hell with cousins and grandmothers. Zoe was going to finish school and move to New Zealand.

Taylor tapped Zoe on the shoulder. "Nickel for your thoughts."

"It's supposed to be a penny."

"First, they don't make pennies in Canada anymore, and second, those looked like some high-end thoughts."

"Let's go find where the band is performing."

"Look. She's gone. The coast is clear. Go talk to him and see if he can help with our project." Taylor turned to leave.

"Wait, where are you going?"

"Zoe, I know you've known him since you were born, but I find him a little creepy. Not perv-creepy. Not at all. More, *What's that under the bed; Don't meet him in a dark alley* creepy."

"But he's not."

"What about the time he came to pick us up at Leslie's party, and her brother's friends were hassling us? All he did was smile at them, and they got all nervous and left."

"He was in uniform and he's built like a wall. They probably thought he was a cop or something."

"Mmm-hmm. Not buying it. It was the creepiness. They felt it and ran. And he's always calling you coo-coo."

"Not coo-coo. *Koukla* or *koukla mou*. It's Greek. It means doll or my little dolly. Honestly, I think he calls all the girls *koukla*, so he doesn't have to remember anyone's name." Zoe led Taylor through the crowded tables.

They walked up behind him. Zoe put her hand on his shoulder. "Uncle Theo?"

Thanatos turned. A big grin on his face. Taylor shuddered, but he didn't seem to notice. "Zoe! *Koukla mou!*" He jumped up and kissed her on both cheeks. She gave him a big hug. He still pronounced her name the Greek way, so it rhymed with joy. He still had a really deep voice for someone who wasn't that tall. And he still wore too much cologne. In other words, it was the perfect hug.

"Uncle Theo, you remember my friend Taylor?"

"Of course." He kissed Taylor's cheeks. She stiffened. "Sit, sit. Do you want chocolate or soda?" He reached into his pocket.

"It's okay." Taylor bounced from her chair. "I'll get it. Would you like another cup of coffee, sir? Something to eat?"

"Just a coffee. Thank you." They watched Taylor make her way to the counter with the longest line.

"She's a nice girl, *Koukla*. Your grandmother likes her very much."

Zoe smiled. He'd lived all these years in Canada and he still confused his verb tenses. Or maybe he missed her grandparents as much as she did. "So, Uncle Theo. How are you? And everyone at the house?"

"Oh, you know, if we were as wise as we were old, we'd be too perfect for this world." He put the crushed napkin into his paper cup and closed the lid. "What about you and your mama? Is everything good? How is school?"

She shrugged. "It's school." She looked up at him from beneath her lashes. "Actually, you might be able to help me with something."

"Someone giving you trouble? You tell me, right, I'll make sure there's no more trouble with this person."

She wondered if the offer extended to newly discovered members of the family. "No worries Uncle Theo. Everything is fine." Taylor arrived carrying a plastic tray of drinks and a large plate of french fries. "Thanks, Tay." She opened a small packet of mayonnaise and emptied it onto the edge of the plate. "Taylor and I are working on a project about Grandpa Eddie and Grandma Rose. And since you worked for them for so long..."

"You must have a lot of stories about them." Taylor sipped her tea.

"I have lots of stories. Wonderful stories. And some of them might even be true."

"So, you'll help us?" Zoe leaned forward.

"Some things are better left secret, *Koukla*." He patted Zoe's hand. "But I'll help if I can."

"Like... what do you know about my cousin?"

"Your cousin?" Thanatos thought for a moment, then chuckled. "Yes, your cousin. Autumn, your cousin. She's a nice girl. You'll like her. You'll meet, and it will be like you've known each other your whole entire lives."

"But what about her parents? Did you know about Rose's other family?"

"Ah, *Koukla*. Autumn Rose had a hard time with her family. Her mother died when she was very, very little."

"So, you've met her before?"

"Maybe, a long time ago. I'm not sure. I was the last to come to the household. And I am just a simple driver, taking people from here to there. There is Kali. She is Autumn Rose's godmother. She would know more. Or you can talk to Autumn. She probably needs to know as much about you as you do about her. You know?"

"I guess we were a surprise to her, too." Zoe tapped her plastic stir stick against the table.

"Mr. Theo? When did you start working for the Sterlings?"

He struck a dramatic pose. "It was a dark and stormy night... or not." Thanatos chuckled as he emptied a packet of sugar into his coffee. "I started working for Mrs. Rose before she was even married. She loved to take long drives out of the city. We'd pack some food and her drawing things and choose a direction."

Zoe had a hard time picturing her grandmother as a young girl, as a carefree artist.

Thanatos smiled as he stirred his coffee. "I remember the first time I had to drive your grandfather by himself. We had an argument. He was ready to fire me. But in the end, we shared a laugh and a beer."

"What happened?" asked Zoe.

"Your grandfather was not used to having a big house with butlers and drivers, and it took him a long, long time to relax around us. Your great-grandmother, Mrs. Sterling, she loved that her son was rich and had a chauffeur. And Mr. Eddie worried about his mama, especially after she became a widow, so I would drive for her, too. She loved it, and she always wanted the biggest car. She would call me to drive her to the corner store, and she made sure all of her neighbors saw when I came to get her. Always wore a mink jacket; summer, and winter— even over her house dress. She was a funny lady."

"Uncle Theo?"

"Sorry, the argument. It was the middle of the 1970s. One of your grandfather's best and oldest customers made very fancy and expensive dresses, and he was having a fashion show in the downtown. It was going to be at a discotheque that was very new and very popular. Mr. Eddie didn't care about fashion shows, but the man had been a very good friend to the gallery and the art group, and he had told some of his rich customers about the fashion show, so he had to go. Your mama had a cold, and your grandmother worried a lot about sickness and didn't want to leave little Nora with anyone else. Her mother had died of sickness when Mrs. Rose was very little.

"There were supposed to be newspaper reporters writing about the show and filming it for television, so Mrs. Rose tells Mr. Eddie the parking will be very bad, and he shouldn't drive himself. Your grandfather gets into the car and tells me the address of this new discotheque. I tell him it's not possible and ask for the address again. He tells me again. I tell him, politely, he's wrong. He shows me the invitation. I say no. We argue."

"What was the matter with the address?" asked Taylor.

"I knew the place as a funeral home, not a discotheque. He thought I was joking. But I say to him, 'I, Thanatos, never joke about funeral homes.' I took my map book, and I showed him. So he becomes nervous. What if he doesn't see his friend's show? Or, worse, what if the printer made a mistake on the invitations, and all of these clients come to a funeral home expecting to see a fashion show? His friend would be embarrassed. Maybe even ruined.

"I say, 'Calm yourself, Mr. Eddie.' I say, 'We'll go to the address and see. If your friend needs help to move the people to the right address, I will bring them back and forth as many times as they need to. He calms down, and we go to the address on the card."

"Which was it?" asked Zoe.

"Son of a gun—it was a discotheque. No more 'rest in peace'. Just boom, boom, boom."

The girls laughed. "What did Grandpa do?"

"He went in and met his friend and saw an excellent fashion show. But he said all through the show he expected someone to bring coffins onto the stage." Thanatos sipped his coffee. "That would be a show I would like to see."

"Honestly?" Zoe said with a giggle.

"Of course, *Koukla*. I like zombie movies. A zombie fashion show would be the only way you would get me to watch people walk back and forth, showing clothes."

"Is that why she is shopping alone?" Zoe asked.

"Who?"

Zoe rolled her eyes. Thanatos shook his head. "Your cousin wanted to see the mall by herself. She has a lot to get used to, the house, the city, everything about this new life. And remember, *Koukla mou*, she has to get used to you being her cousin as much as you need to get used to her being yours."

Zoe shrugged.

Thanatos sighed. "Zoe, *Koukla mou*, she is not a bad person, and she loved her family, but they're gone. She knows how you feel. How about I telephone you when she is finished shopping, and if you're ready too, I can drive you and your friend home?"

Zoe nodded as she and Taylor stood up. "I'll speak to you later, Uncle Theo." She kissed his cheek and left the food court.

"Well?" said Taylor.

"The meeting wasn't a total loss. We got a good story for our project."

"Ooh, zombie fashion models. I like it!"

"Let's go see if *Polka-Dot Death-Shroud* is still around."

hanatos found Autumn sitting on a bench, casually watching people's *Ka* communicate with their hosts. It fascinated her to see how much they interacted without the person realizing how they were being influenced. Some advised on purchases. Others studied for upcoming exams while their hosts strolled by the shops. One *Ka*, a brain-numbed look of annoyance on her face, broke into a tap-dance routine while her host listened to an older woman, who kept showing photos of something on her phone. The older woman's *Ka* kept reminding her host of things to point out in the photo. The other *Ka* expanded its repertoire from Ginger

Rogers to Riverdance. The *Ka*'s jumps and twirls were very impressive. Autumn disguised her laugh as a cough.

Thanatos sat down beside her.

"Uncle Theo, this is almost as bad as being able to read people's minds."

"That's what makes it so much fun. But *Koukla*, you can't just sit here and wait for a *Ka* to come and tell you they need help."

"I'm not. I was planning to go into that store." Thanatos picked up a free parenting magazine. "Uncle Theo, aren't you coming?"

"No. You'll be fine."

"But I might be a while."

"Don't worry, Autumn." He opened the magazine. "I'm very patient."

Autumn went into the store and pulled a short dress from the rack. The print reminded her of something she'd seen before. A wallpaper pattern in one of the disused rooms? A dress she'd found in one of the storage boxes?

"Bonjour, hi." The salesgirl had a rosy, round face and a warm smile. "Est-ce que je peux t'aider? Can I help you?"

Autumn looked up and was about to answer when she noticed Kali floating beside the girl's knee. Her nametag read Claire. Autumn didn't know what to say. She focused on the dress in her hand. "This is pretty."

"Isn't it? The whole line was done in patterns taken from vintage Art Deco textiles. All those wonderful colors and shapes, and still a hundred percent machine washable." She looked around the store. "And I have a gorgeous pair of leggings in either Harvest Gold or Gas Blue to go with it. Aren't those great names? Would you like to try them on?"

"Yeah, sounds great." Autumn looked outside the store, but Thanatos wasn't anywhere to be seen.

"Is everything okay?"

"My uncle was waiting for me. He must have gone to get a cup of coffee." Claire looked to be the picture of health, but her *Ka* told a different story. "I guess that gives me more time to shop." Autumn smiled and hoped it looked sincere. Claire's *Ka* had bags beneath its eyes and was half Claire's weight. When the *Ka* turned, Autumn saw a green pulsing mass just above her left ear, buried inside its head. Maybe an aneurysm or brain tumor? Autumn hoped her smile looked authentic. "I'm having a hard time deciding on whether to get a dress or a skirt."

"We have some nice skirts over here if you'd like to have a look." Claire picked up a pair of blue leggings and led Autumn deeper into the store.

Autumn casually put her hand into her jacket pocket, feeling for the ghost stone. She felt the silky oil on the tips of her fingers.

Claire held up a print skirt and a jersey T-shirt that matched one of the colors in the pattern. "What do you think?"

Autumn's hand brushed Claire's as she reached for the hanger. "That's so pretty. Can I try on both outfits?" A warm feeling spread up Autumn's arm.

Claire's *Ka* stumbled with surprise. "Of course," Claire said with a smile. "The changing rooms are this way." Claire's *Ka* became more solid and lost its silver hue. It kissed Claire's cheek and whispered something into her ear. It turned away from the salesgirl, spread its arms out like wings, and flew through a wall, out into the unknown.

Autumn waited for some kind of reaction. For Claire to notice her *Ka* had left.

"Do you still want to try these on?" Claire gathered the hangers and draped the clothes over her arm.

"Sorry. Just lost in thought. Let's go find me some new outfits" Autumn followed Claire to the dressing room, looking to see if the *Ka* was hiding somewhere close.

"So, where are you interning?" Claire asked

Autumn waited for Claire to explode or panic or break down into tears. But she didn't look or act any different. "I'm not interning anywhere. I'm starting at a new high school in a bit. Why did you think I was going to work?"

"High school? How old are you?"

"I'm sixteen."

"Sixteen, okay. It's the clothes, they're… Well, never mind."

"Come on Claire."

"It's just these clothes will make you look older, you know, more serious, and that's not the impression you want to give at a new school."

"That could be a problem. I guess you should just put them back." Autumn could sense a change in Claire, and she knew it had nothing to do with her missing *Ka*. "I have a confession to make." She took a step closer to Claire and looked around to see if anyone was listening. "I have no idea how I'm supposed to dress. My late father had me dress very conservatively, and my guardian hasn't looked at a fashion magazine since Princess Di's funeral. My uncle has such a good heart. He took pity on my stunted wardrobe and brought me to the mall. I guess I wore school uniforms for so long, I forgot what fashion looks like. To be honest, I'm feeling completely overwhelmed. A new city. A new school. Now, a new wardrobe. I have absolutely no idea what to get. Will you be my hero, Claire? Can you help a girlfriend out?"

Claire's smile reached all the way to her toes. "Let's add these to make the guardian happy and keep your uncle out of trouble. But we're going over to that side of the store. By the time we're finished, you're going to look lit."

Autumn stood at the cash. Four huge shopping bags filled the counter. Two more rested by her ankles. Claire handed back Autumn's credit card just as Thanatos came into the store.

"Hello Autumn," he said. "I was getting worried." He looked at all the bags. "So, have you worn the numbers off the card yet?"

"Not quite, Uncle Theo, but I gave them a good polishing." She picked up a few bags, and he reached for the rest. Thanatos smiled at Claire. She blushed as if he flirted.

*Curiouser and curiouser,* thought Autumn. *Maybe those without a Ka see Death differently.*

Another salesgirl came up behind Claire. She nodded a greeting to Autumn and Thanatos. "Claire, can you take my shift next weekend?"

Claire thought for a moment. "No. I've decided to head out east and visit my grandparents that weekend."

"Come on. You can visit them another time. Please?"

"No." She turned to her coworker and gave her a look that could peel paint. "Work your own shift."

The other girl grumbled and went to find someone else to cover for her.

"I'm sorry," Claire said, smiling shyly. "She should have waited to speak to me."

"Does she always try to get you to cover her weekends?" Autumn asked.

Claire sighed, "Pretty much. Ah, well, she won't be my problem much longer." Autumn looked puzzled. Claire laughed. "I don't know where that came from. Maybe I'll extend my weekend and visit with my family for a while. I love Ville des Saintes, but it's not really my home. You know what I mean?"

"I think I do." Autumn lifted her bags. "Safe travels."

"Thank you, and thank you for shopping at Boutique L&M."

Autumn and Thanatos carried the bags out of the store. He adjusted his grip on one of the handles. "Autumn, if you buy everything our, um, customers have to sell, you will spend everything your father and Rose left for your future."

"I needed some new clothes. Everything in my closet must be about fifty years old or looks like I should be fifty years old."

"You loved those older jeans and dresses and wouldn't part with them. And the newer clothes, they were chosen during a shopping trip with your godmother. So, I would be careful how you talk about those things."

"I'll tell her the truth. My conscience needed to be soothed for what I did to her by getting her a good commission."

"Just this one time. Otherwise, we will need a bigger house."

That was it. The moment Zoe decided she hated Autumn. Others might call them cousins, but Autumn wasn't Zoe's family. It wasn't enough that Autumn had taken the necklace she admired and the house she'd practically grown up in. *Her alleged cousin* wasn't even waiting for the headstone to be up before she spent all her grandmother's money. She was laughing with the salesgirl. Laughing! How could she be so happy when Zoe's heart was so broken?

"Zoe?" Taylor gently laid her hand on Zoe's shoulder. "How about we grab a hot chocolate and call my mom for a ride home?"

Zoe nodded. She didn't trust herself to speak. And if this horrible ache didn't heal soon, she may never speak again.

utumn looked at herself in the bedroom mirror. She practiced greeting her aunt and cousin for the fourth time. She tried a closed-lip smile, then one which showed too many teeth. Both said less *happy to meet you* and more *maybe the second bean burrito was a mistake*. The formal greeting her father had taught her felt stiff. The "Hi, how are ya?" felt insincere. The "Yo! What's up?" she'd witnessed at the mall felt idiotic. Maybe she should just stay home.

There was a knock at the door. "*Beti*, may I come in?"

"Of course Auntie-ji." Autumn sat down heavily on the bed. She pasted on a smile. Kali had tried to discourage her from going tonight. If she saw Autumn having second thoughts, she would cancel the dinner for Autumn's own good.

"What's the matter, *Beti*? You don't look very excited to become acquainted with your family."

Autumn sighed. "It's not that. I went through the whole mall yesterday—twice—thinking about what to get for Nora and Zoe. I worked with the ghosts, and Thanatos showed me how to recognize people's *Ka* and how to help them, but this first meeting was always at the back of my mind. Everything looked so unimportant, so insignificant. I mean, how could I go in to meet my long-lost family and hand them kitchen towels or a potted plant? Am I making sense?"

Suddenly, Autumn noticed Kali holding the jewelry box. "Auntie-ji?"

"I thought this would answer the problem."

Autumn set the box on the bed and opened it. "Auntie-ji, I know some of these pieces belonged to my mother, Elizabeth."

"And some of them belonged to Rose. If you wish, I could remove the enchantment from those pieces."

"So I could give them to Nora and Zoe as mementos? Brilliant!"

"A very special gesture and a nice gift *Beti*. Do you know which things you'd like to give away?"

Autumn picked up a pair of Elizabeth's garnet earrings. There was a locket with Autumn's initials engraved on it: "A.R.C.". Were there clues to her history inside? She held her breath as she opened it. There was a photo of a woman on one side and a young girl on the other. But she didn't know who they were. A memory tickled something at the back of her mind, but she asked Kali about them just the same.

"The woman on the left is Rose's daughter, Nora. The little girl is her daughter, Zoe. These are old photos, *Beti*."

Autumn put the locket down. It wasn't her locket. It belonged to Rose, her grandmother. She forgot they shared the same initials. She'd have her own photos to put in there someday, she hoped.

Autumn picked up the crescent moon she had worn to the mall. The moon was platinum with white and yellow gold accents done in an Art Deco style on a white gold chain. There was a gold brooch in a sunburst pattern, bracelets and bangles, and three more pairs of earrings. Autumn felt someone watching her from the shadows.

"Have you made your decision?"

"Umm, Auntie-ji? Are there any small boxes or something I can use to wrap the jewelry?"

"Of course. I'll get them for you." Her eyes slid to the corner of the room. "It might allow you to get inspired, to think things through."

Autumn stood up and closed the door behind Kali. She turned

around, scanning the room. "Hello Mr. Ghost, it's nice to meet you. It's okay if you don't want to show yourself just yet. I understand."

She sat on the bed. "I guess you've been listening to what's been going on." She spread the jewelry out in front of her. "Can you please help me choose what to give to Nora and Zoe?" She watched the bed, hoping something would float up and into her hand. Nothing. She looked around for some other sign, then remembered her radio.

The ghost had been able to mess with it before. She turned it on. All she heard was loud music. Maybe she should get out the ghost stone? Or maybe just ask a clear question.

"Which piece should I give to Zoe?" The song didn't change. Maybe the answer would be on another channel, or she might hear something in the static. She tried moving the dial on the radio.

She slowly changed the station. She got to a classical music station, but the control stuck. "Is this the clue?" She took her hand off the radio and listened. A gentle piano piece played, slow and haunting. Autumn had heard the song before, and she hummed along. Suddenly, she remembered the song's name: *Claire du Lune*.

Lune: the French word for "moon". Zoe would get the crescent moon necklace. Autumn put the pendant on the dresser. This was too cool.

She sat down on the bed again. "Thank you, Mr. Ghost. Now, what should I choose for Nora?" She moved the knob on the radio again. It got stuck on an old disco song with a heavy, discordant guitar. "Mr. Ghost, I don't understand that clue at all."

She closed her eyes as she felt the room tilt sideways. Her stomach lurched, and Autumn was glad she was sitting. Someone whispered, *"Dance with me, Rosie."*

Autumn opened her eyes. She found herself standing at the bedroom door. The older couple from the nightmare appeared in the room, frozen mid-step. They looked younger than in the car accident. Somehow, she knew it was the late 1980s. As if a director yelled "Action", they began to move.

Eddie stormed around the bedroom. "I'm putting a padlock on that door!" He pointed accusingly at the bedroom's second closet. "No, two! Two padlocks. And I won't even tell you the combination."

"I don't see the problem." Rose tried not to laugh. "It's not like you have nothing to wear."

"Now, but it won't stay that way. Watch. First it was my sweaters, then my sports coats. She'll be stealing my underwear next!"

Their seventeen-year-old daughter, Nora, swung into her parents' bedroom. She wore tight black leggings tucked into Rose's short leather boots. She'd pinned an enamel flamingo to Eddie's herringbone jacket, worn with the sleeves rolled up. She'd pushed his fedora down over her teased and lacquered hair. "Daddykins, you're overreacting. You've got to keep it mellow." His jacket slipped open. Nora was wearing one of his undershirts.

Eddie sat down heavily on the bed. "My clothes will never be safe again."

Nora grabbed a pair of hoop earrings and a large cuff from Rose's tray. "Borrowing these." She blew kisses in their direction and danced out of the room.

Rose put her head on Eddie's shoulder. "I'm sure she'll grow out of it dear. Don't worry."

He looked back at Rose, a lopsided smirk on his face. "She doesn't have to grow out of it too fast, does she?"

Autumn watched Nora bounce down the stairs, singing about walking like an Egyptian, the song on her radio.

She snapped back to the twenty-first century, carrying with her the love Rose felt for her family. It made Autumn feel more determined to meet them, to experience that feeling for herself. On her bed, leaning against a pair of gold hoops, she saw the bracelet from her vision. It was a gold cuff set with alternating light blue and pink rectangular tourmaline stones.

Autumn picked it up and put it beside the moon pendant. "Thank you, Mr. Ghost. I hope we can talk again soon."

*Z*oe had thought up a million reasons to leave the house for the evening, but her mother hadn't bought any of them. She was stuck having dinner with the girl previously known as *the cousin.*

Nora had rearranged all the knickknacks, twice. This time Zoe caught her mother moving the candy dish for the 500th time. So far, Zoe found it on the dining room table, on the entry table in the hall, and now on the end table by the sofa. It became a game, like hide-and-seek, or find the random objects hidden in a picture.

The dish had been in her grandparents' home for as long as she could remember. It had a place of honor on her grandfather's desk. He used to call it the most precious artwork he owned. Zoe could never figure out why. The colors and the abstract flower design were nice, but the uneven clay made it wobble a bit. The shape was off, not quite oval, but too egg-shaped to be round, higher on one side than the other. There were permanent drip marks in the finish where the glaze was put on too thick. Initials had been cut into the bottom along with a date, but Zoe couldn't read either of those.

Grandpa Eddie always had a soft spot for folk art. It didn't matter if it was a weird candy dish or a life-sized papier-mâché Mountie or an angel carved into an axe handle, he saw beauty in the simplest of things.

Zoe came back from her bedroom to find Nora still rearranging photos, only now they were being moved by millimeters. Zoe rolled her eyes and went to brush her hair.

"Zoe, did you finish setting the table?"

"Yes!" She'd have to be careful. Nora's nervous energy was catching. Zoe took a deep breath. This was her home, her mother's dinner party. Nothing to worry about. They were Sterlings, united against one gate-crashing Cassidy. Autumn Rose might be blood, but she wasn't family. And Zoe could always find a reason to leave the apartment early and go downstairs to Taylor's.

Nora stood at the bedroom door. "We'll be calm and welcoming. We'll meet her and find out what she plans to do..."

"Besides running through Grandma's money at warp-speed?"

"Zoe, please. Can you leave your attitude in your room for just this one night? You can go back to making Autumn-shaped voodoo dolls tomorrow. I promise. Just give me this one night."

"I don't know." She tapped her hairbrush against her leg. "I'm almost out of cotton batting to make the dolls. It's going to be difficult to tell my cousin to get stuffed without cotton batting."

Nora smirked. "We'll get some more tomorrow." She kissed her daughter's cheek.

The phone rang. It was Pierre in the lobby. Autumn Rose Cassidy, long-lost cousin, and bane of her existence, was on her way up.

<br>

*A*utumn watched the numbers change as she passed each floor, the two velvet jewelry bags tucked safely into her purse. She held a cake box with both hands. Maybe she should have chosen a chocolate cake instead of bringing a strawberry shortcake. Why didn't she get the chocolate cake? Or should she have chosen a pie?

What should she call her grandmother's daughter? Mrs. Williams? She was divorced. Ms. Sterling? Aunt Nora? Should she shake their hands when they meet? Should she expect a hug? Should she offer one?

She took a deep breath. "Autumn. Get a hold of yourself. You're going to make yourself crazy. Cake is cake. You encounter death every single day, you can meet your grandmother's family."

The doors of the elevator opened on the twelfth floor. Autumn had passed the point of no return.

Autumn knocked on the door. Maybe Kali was right. Maybe it was too soon. Maybe she'd made a mistake coming here. What if they asked her questions about her past, and Autumn couldn't remember the answers? Should she lie and pretend everything was hunky-dory? Should she tell them about her memory problem? Maybe she should call Uncle Theo and just go home.

The door opened, and an older version of herself smiled at her. "Autumn? Hello. I'm your Aunt Nora. Please come in."

The hallway opened into three archways. Through the one on her left, she could see a small kitchen. The largest archway was straight ahead, and it led into a living room with a fantastic view of the whole of Snowy Hill. A girl about her own age leaned against the wall leading to a longer hallway. Her hair was the same as Autumn's, her eyes were like those of the man from her vision, but the shape of her face and her skin tone reminded Autumn of her father.

Nora took the girl's hand and pulled her close. "Autumn, this is your cousin Zoe."

Zoe nodded and pulled her phone from her pocket. "Sorry, I have to take this. Important school project." She turned and walked back down the long hall.

"She usually keeps her phone on vibrate and..." Nora sounded a bit flustered.

Zoe's phone rang for real as she pretended to be talking into it. Nora's look spoke volumes, a whole library's worth. There was comedy, perhaps some drama, and one was definitely a murder mystery.

"I like that song," Autumn said as she passed Nora the cake box. "Zoe's ringtone? *Hard Day's Night*. I like that song."

"So did my father. He liked all types of music, but his favorite was classic rock and roll. Zoe would never have learned about The Beatles if it weren't for him and a very old cassette recorder he let her use." Nora thanked her for the cake and showed Autumn into the living room. "Dinner will be ready soon. I have some crudités prepared. I'll be back in a minute."

"You have a nice home," Autumn called out as she walked around the room. There was a mix of antique and modern pieces. Everything was arranged into set-design perfection. The small café table had been set for dinner. It was more intimate than the dining room, with its mahogany furniture and massive crystal chandelier.

Autumn saw a small clay candy dish and picked it up. It seemed so familiar. She knew she'd seen it before, but she didn't know where she'd seen it or how she knew it. Something to do with summer camp. Autumn set it down as Nora came in with a tray of cut vegetables and dip.

"I saw you looking at the bowl. What do you think?"

"It's pretty."

"Thank you." Nora smiled. "I made it when I was eight, my first trip to sleep-away camp. The way my father praised it, you'd think he was going to send it to the Louvre or the Guggenheim." She stood beside Autumn. "To tell you the truth, I'd forgotten about it until I found it in his office after he... after they..." Nora cleared her throat.

"I understand." Autumn turned to look at the art on the wall over the sofa. "What about this painting?" Autumn could name the painter, and she knew the work. She could even picture the street depicted in the piece, but she couldn't say how she knew any of it.

The painting was a winter scene. The hood of a black car was just visible in front of an outdoor iron staircase. A red brick storefront dominated the painting. Its white awning advertised tobacco and magazines. A sign in the store window reminded onlookers that tea and coffee were rationed.

"My father said he'd been raised in a grocery store like the one in the painting," Nora said. "His parents ran the store, and the family lived in an apartment in the back." Nora smiled. "It's not *Sterling's Family Grocery*, but my dad said it was close enough. Harvey Workman, the artist, presented it to my father as a gift for his fortieth birthday."

Nora put the tray of cut vegetables and dip down on the coffee table. "Harvey Workman was the first to join *The Crayon Box Collective* and the first of its members to die. Cancer took him way too soon. His loss was very hard on my parents." She sighed. "Last year, my father was offered a million dollars for this painting. But he wouldn't even consider selling it. He said it reminded him of where he came from."

Nora called Zoe. Dinner was almost ready. "I hope you like lasagna, Autumn. I've been trying to perfect my father's spaghetti sauce."

Zoe sat down beside Autumn and put a carrot stick into the dip. "My mom's is good, but it's not like Grandpa Eddie's."

"I'm determined. I'll figure it out." Nora's carrot crunched her resolve's exclamation point.

In Autumn's mind's eye, she saw a tall man with graying hair and blue eyes standing behind a kitchen counter, a chaos of empty tomato paste tins, whole tomato jars, and vegetable peelings strewn around him. Bill Haley and the Comets played in the background. Eddie pressed his lips together in concentration as he cut all the vegetables and fed them into the food processor. There was tomato sauce on his blue polo shirt.

He looked up from the cutting board and smiled at Autumn. "The secret is the vegetables. If they're ground up enough, Zoe will never know they're there." He wiped his hand on a kitchen towel. "It worked on Nora, it'll work on her daughter too."

He cursed at the lid of the processor when it stuck. The extra energy helped open the bowl, and he spooned the mashed celery, peppers, mushrooms, and carrots into his 'world famous' spaghetti sauce.

Nora touched Autumn's hand. "Are you okay? You seemed lost for a moment."

Autumn nodded and reached for a slice of green pepper. All of the vegetables Eddie had used in his sauce were there on the tray. "Have you ever tried processing vegetables and adding them to the sauce?"

"Have you ever had my grandfather's spaghetti sauce?" Zoe asked.

"I don't know. I mean, I don't remember. Maybe." Autumn shrugged. "It was just a thought."

"Since you didn't know my grandparents, your opinion doesn't mean much. Does it?" Zoe took two pieces of pepper and crunched them loudly.

"You might actually be onto something Autumn," Nora said. My parents always tried to sneak vegetables into me, one way or another. And pasta was my greatest weakness. It makes sense. That's what he must have used. I'm going to have to try using vegetables in my next batch."

"Joy of joys," Zoe said without much emotion. "One mystery solved." She looked sideways at Autumn. "So many more to go."

Nora shot her daughter a look that could have made Kali uncomfortable. "Zoe, please come help me in the kitchen."

Zoe might have wanted to give a snarky reply, but something in her mother's tone made her rise obediently.

"We'll just be a moment." Nora smiled and led Zoe out of the room.

Autumn looked around the room with her Kali pendant in her fist. The ghost from Rowan House was nowhere to be seen or felt.

An older woman wearing a white mink jacket waved at her from the entranceway. "Autumn Rose, it's been too long since we've visited." Grandmother Sterling smiled. "Not to worry about the girls, lovey. I've been watching over my granddaughter and my great-granddaughter since I left. You might want to watch your daughter more closely, lovey. Her heart's been broken, just like my sweet husband. And that Zoe. She's a bit of a spitfire. Beware though. She's got the gift. I can see it in her eyes." The woman winked and faded into the mirror's reflected light.

Before she could ask the woman about what she'd said, harsh whispers came from the kitchen. Maybe Kali was right. They weren't ready to meet her or welcome her into their family. Autumn was mad at herself. She should know by now that families are overrated. It didn't matter, with her memory, she'd forget them soon anyway.

Her very own family.

It was a nice thought while it lasted.

Autumn took the two velvet bags from her purse and put them on the coffee table. She started for the door, taking her coat off the chair. She'd wander around downtown until she got hungry, then grab a burger. When a reasonable amount of time had passed, she'd come back to the building and call Uncle Theo to come and pick her up. Hopefully, Kali wouldn't ask too many questions about how the evening went.

Nora popped her head out of the kitchen just as Autumn reached for the doorknob. "Were you leaving?"

"I'm sorry." Autumn swallowed back the lump in her throat.

"Madam Kali said it was probably too soon for us to meet. I never intended to cause anyone any discomfort. It might be easier if I left." She tried to smile through the tears in her eyes. "You have a lovely home. Thank you for inviting me."

"Please wait." Nora put the oven mitts on the counter. "Zoe, where are you?"

Zoe came into the hallway from the living room. She had the two velvet bags in her hands. "What are these?"

"Madam Kali told me they belonged to Rose, so I thought you'd like to have them as mementos of her."

"At least come back in while we open your gifts." Nora took Autumn's coat and led her back to the living room.

Autumn sat at the edge of a wingback chair while Nora and Zoe sat down on the sofa.

"I hope you like them. I wasn't sure what you'd like. But you can say these pieces kind of spoke to me."

Nora pulled out the bracelet. "I haven't seen this in I don't remember how long..." She laughed and brushed away a stray tear. "I got this for my mother when I was ten. I chose it for her birthday."

Zoe smiled. "You signed your name to the birthday card, and your father signed his name to the credit card."

Nora laughed. "I saved up my allowance to buy it. It cost me everything in my piggy bank—a whole four dollars and twenty-seven cents." She shrugged. "Okay, so my father may have helped, just a little." Nora slipped on the cuff. "What did Autumn bring you, Zoe?"

Zoe opened the bag's drawstring. She found the chain and pulled out the crescent moon pendant. It swung in a small circle like a pendulum answering an unasked question.

"I remember that necklace," Nora said as she held the pendant in her hand for a moment. "My father bought it for my mother in an antique store when they were on their honeymoon. Zoe was always begging to wear it when she played dress-up. Do you remember Zoe?"

Zoe nodded, then cleared her throat. "Thank you, Autumn." She slipped the necklace over her head.

"It was very thoughtful," Nora said.

"You're most welcome." Autumn moved to sit more comfortably on the chair.

Zoe looked at her as if she were part of a portrait study.

Nora stood up. "The lasagna is out of the oven, and I have some finishing touches to add to the salad. I'll be back in a moment, and we'll have dinner. You'll be staying, I hope?"

Autumn nodded. Zoe moved closer to the end of the sofa, so she and Autumn sat closer together. She pulled her phone out of her pocket and looked at the screen. She glanced over at Autumn, then back at the phone. Zoe shut it off and lay it face down on the coffee table.

"Thanks again. For the necklace, I mean."

"You're welcome." They sat in silence.

Zoe passed Autumn the tray. "Would you like another?"

Autumn took a carrot and thanked her. The only sound was the crunching of vegetables. They both started to speak, apologized, and waited for the other to say something. Silence reigned again.

"Where are you from?" Zoe asked. "I mean, you have a bit of an accent."

"I was born in India, but my father sent me to England after my mother died. I was about nine when we came to Canada."

"I'm guessing you don't have any siblings. I mean, there aren't any other cousins I should know about?" Zoe asked

"There's just me. My father remarried, and I have a stepbrother somewhere in the world. When my father passed away a little over four years ago, my stepmother and her son packed themselves up, and I never heard from either of them again."

"That's terrible! Your step-monster sounds like mine—a real sweetheart." She leaned toward Autumn. "Don't tell my mother, but mine actually sent me an email saying my father has a new family now and not to expect anything from him anymore: no holiday cards, no birthday gifts, and no appearances at big events like my high school graduation or my wedding."

"That's unspeakable!" She felt protective of her new cousin. Autumn was ready to borrow Kali's sword and slice the horrible woman into a jigsaw puzzle. "You have to tell your mother and show her the email. Let her get her lawyer involved. I'll even help you find a recipe for slow-roasted bitch."

Zoe laughed, "Easy there. You don't even know these people."

"I'm sorry. It's just I would hate to see you hurt by your stepmother in the same way as I was hurt by mine."

Nora called them to the table. Zoe filled the water glasses. Everything looked wonderful and smelled heavenly.

"May I propose a toast?" Autumn said. The others lifted their glasses. "To my hostesses. Thank you for this invitation. To the health and happiness of my newfound family."

Zoe smiled. "And to the early demise of our step-bitches." Nora looked at her questioningly. "Autumn has one like mine."

Nora nodded. "And to Rose Cassidy Sterling, the woman who brought us all together." They sipped their water. Nora lifted the spatula. "Now, let's dig in."

Zoe flopped onto her bed. She'd seen Nora sneak her after-dinner heart medication when she went to prepare dessert. Now her mom was driving Autumn home. The dishwasher was loaded and running. All the leftovers were in the fridge.

She lifted the pendant and gave it a quick kiss. "She looks like you, Grandma. She pushes her hair out of the way and gestures when she talks, just the way Mom and I do. She even brought us our favorite dessert without even knowing it. But, Grandma, I still don't know what to make of her."

Zoe's computer started singing Lionel Richie's song *Hello*. Taylor's face appeared as soon as Zoe hit the button.

"So? Do you need me to come upstairs to your place? Is everything calm? And more importantly, how bad do we hate her?"

"And a very good evening to you too, Taylor." Zoe moved the laptop onto the bed and adjusted the camera. "Dinner wasn't terrible."

"So, we don't hate her?"

"She's an orphan whose stepmother abandoned her when she was twelve. She's lived in three countries, but never had a place to call home."

"So, we feel sorry for her?"

"Look what she gave me." Zoe held the pendant up to the camera. "It was my grandmother's. Grandpa Eddie bought it for her in Paris."

"Okay. We like her."

Nora called Zoe from the hallway.

"In here Mom."

"Thanks for straightening up the kitchen, honey." Nora pointed to the back of the computer. "Taylor?"

"Hello Aunt Nora!"

"Hello Taylor. Please tell your mom I'll meet her in the parking garage in the morning."

"Will do."

"By the way, honey. Autumn and I were talking in the car. It seems she's not registered for school. So, Tuesday morning, I'll be registering her at Saint Kate's."

"But that's where I go to school."

"I know Zoe," Nora said. "It means she'll have someone to show her the ropes." Nora turned to leave. "Don't stay up too late girls."

Zoe opened her mouth to say something to her mother, but nothing came out. She thought for a moment. She looked back at Taylor. "What just happened?"

"So... we hate her again?"

The bus stopped at the public parking lot near the base of Snowy Hill. Autumn got off and walked to the path leading to the summit. She wore a pair of small gold hoops in her ears, one of the pieces of jewelry Kali had enchanted to replace the ones she had given to Nora and Zoe.

It seemed lately she and Kali just had one argument after another. Autumn had questions, and Kali would become impatient as if Autumn should know everything. But how was she supposed to remember things that happened years ago, when she couldn't remember what happened last month?

Autumn began climbing the steps that would take her to the parks on the upper part of the Hill. Autumn wanted to enchant new pieces of jewelry so she could work with the *Ka* as well as ghosts. That had spurred the most recent argument. Working with *Ka* would be more complicated, but Autumn reminded Kali if she could help the *Ka*, there would be fewer ghosts.

That led to an argument about the jewelry. Autumn had bought a pair of simple gold earrings and had brought them and her grandmother's locket to Kali. But apparently, these pieces weren't good enough.

"*Beti*, these things are made for a girl, someone less important."

"Kali, my grandmother wore this locket. If she wore it and she did this work, the locket is important. As for the earrings, I'm sixteen. All of those other pieces are way too expensive for someone my age. I have to be able to fit in at school."

"School? Which school? You don't go to school."

"I should be going to school. Aunt Nora is going to help me register on Tuesday, after Thanksgiving."

"High school is not important *Beti*. Don't you remember?"

"But I have to think about my future. What about getting a job? Or a career? I can't do either without school."

"You have your future all planned. You have enough wealth to last you the rest of your life, and you have fulfillment from the work you do for me."

"But what about living my life? Meeting people? Finding friends? Finding love?"

"We've discussed this before. Many times. Those types of things are not important to someone like you."

"But Auntie..."

Kali slapped the table. "Enough talking about nonsense. You are not like other girls, and you shouldn't worry about those mortal concerns. For someone like you, school will be nothing but a frivolous waste of time."

"I *am* a mortal girl, so these things *are* my concerns. And if going to school is a frivolous waste of time, it's my time to waste!" Autumn slammed the front door when she left. She'd planned to go to the park on Snowy Hill today anyway. She'd just gone without Uncle Theo.

Would Saint Katherine's Academy of the Arts let her in without a portfolio? Nora was confident she could get into the art history program to start. It would give her a chance to decide what she wanted to specialize in and build an appropriate portfolio.

Autumn breathed in the crisp air as she made her way past the sculptures at the beginning of the park's path. The red and gold leaves spread out before her like an abstract painting. The sky was a particular shade of cyan that made photographers swoon.

A man smiled as he jogged by on the walkway. Three dogs raced through the grass and leaves. A terrier and a toy poodle barked as they chased a German shepherd around the trees. The big dog stopped with his tail wagging, to let his short-legged friends catch up. Two women walked after them, leashes in hand, laughing at their antics.

Autumn chose the path toward the man-made pond known as Otter Lake, climbing higher through the parks. An older man with gray hair and a fine mustache was walking a corgi in the opposite direction. The man bent to adjust the dog's plaid coat. "Come on, Starbuck, there's a good girl." He winced slightly as he straightened up.

The image of Kali hovered over the man's right shoulder. Autumn slipped her hand into her pocket for the oil from the Earth stone.

"Isn't she sweet? May I pat her?" The man nodded. Autumn crouched down beside the dog. "The poor thing." Autumn looked up. "She seems to have something caught in her fur."

The man leaned down again to pull some dead leaves out from beneath the dog's coat, leaves Autumn had put there so she could easily brush the man's exposed wrist.

"I know you are curious about everything, Starbuck," he said, "but no more investigating huge piles of leaves."

Autumn waved goodbye and continued along the path. The man's *Ka* ran past to catch up with its host.

The man turned and waved back. He looked down at the dog. "Come on, Starbuck. You've added enough new fans to your club for today. Let's get home and see what Tim made us for lunch."

Fall was making itself felt. Autumn tightened her scarf. She couldn't smell the coming of snow, but the chill in the air meant it wasn't far off.

City workers and volunteers set up a tarp and boards, waiting for it to get cold enough to create the ice rink. A small truck passed, loaded with hay bales. They headed toward the toboggan run, a safe way to make sure no one sledding down the hill would end up in traffic. Autumn felt as if she saw all this for the first time, but she also knew what everyone was doing, and how everything would look after it was all finished, with the ground covered in snow. It was all new, but she felt she'd been experiencing it for years.

Autumn released people's *Ka* and reattached others. There was satisfaction in knowing there would be fewer lost souls in the city. Living people moved around the hill's paths, sometimes pushing strollers, sometimes jogging, sometimes doing both at the same time.

Out of the corner of her eye, she saw someone in a tuxedo walking on another path. He seemed to be trying to talk to the people around him, but they ignored him. Autumn turned to look at him. There wasn't anyone there. The people were there, yes, but the man in the tuxedo was gone. He couldn't have moved that fast. She scanned the walkways and caught sight of him again in her peripheral vision.

Autumn turned to look at him, and he'd disappeared. She looked away, and he was there in the corner of her eye.

Autumn sighed. He was a ghost. She'd been so focused on *Ka*, she forgot to check the park for ghosts. The poor guy had been trying to talk to everyone on the hill, but no one could see or hear him. So she stopped and waited for him to find her.

"Excuse me, miss, but can you help me, please?"

Autumn nodded and took out her phone. He slumped and started to walk away.

"Hey. Where are you going?" she said.

"Are you speaking to me?" He ran back to where she had stopped. "You can hear me? Really?"

"The reception is pretty clear. If you stop moving around, I'll be able to see you. What's your name?"

"Henry. My name is Henry." He was closer now. Autumn could make out the acne scars on his cheek. He was wearing white gloves, and there was something white on his jacket. She wasn't sure if it was a flower or a pocket square.

"Do you know where I am and why people are ignoring me?" He paced in and out of her vision. "It's just, like, weird, you know? Like, one minute, my friend is texting to get directions to a fancy pool party we're supposed to be working. Next thing, I'm, like, standing in the park, trying to get someone to talk to me."

"Were you driving?"

"Nope. I can. I have my license. And I'm only one hundred dollars away from my very own new, used car."

"But your friend was driving and texting?"

"Yeah. He does it all the time. We were just coming up Snowy Hill. The curve is pretty steep."

"Do you know what happened?"

"No."

"I'm sorry, Henry, but you died."

"Except I'm not dead." He ran his hand through his hair. "I can't be dead. I'm buying a car. I've got a date on Saturday. My parents have a big anniversary in three weeks. I can't be dead!"

He pulled off his gloves and wrung them between his hands. "Please tell me it's just a bad joke." He started to panic. "Please tell me the guys are hiding, waiting for me to freak out so they can post a video of me blubbering. Please tell me it's all a mistake!"

"I'm so sorry."

Henry started to back away. "No! You're wrong! You're lying!"

"Please don't run away. Let me help you."

"No! You're just… wrong!"

"If you believe your friends arranged this to make you look foolish, how did they get everyone on the mountain to cooperate?"

"I… they…" He scrubbed his face with his hands. "What do I do?"

Autumn put some of the ghost stone's potion in her hand and held it out to him. "Put some of this oil on your skin." She felt the tingle as his ghostly fingers brushed her palm.

"Now what?"

"We wait." With the solution in her hand, Autumn could see him clearly, no matter how much he paced.

"Too bad I don't have a deck of cards," Henry said as he leaned against a tree.

"Patience."

They heard someone coming from beneath the trees, whistling *You Are My Sunshine.*

"Do you hear that?" Henry scanned the area. "I know him."

"You should Henry." A gray-haired man with military bearing leaned on a walking stick, more for effect than need. Henry might have looked like him in forty years or so. "I'm your grandfather."

Henry thought for a moment. "You're my mom's father. There's a picture of you on her dresser."

"That's right. We've come to get you and take you to your new home."

"Who's we?" A dog barked in the distance. Henry turned in the direction of the sound. "That sounds like..." Before he could speak again, a chocolate lab galloped out of the woods. It jumped on Henry, knocking him to the ground. "Fudge!" Henry said between dog licks. "It's Fudge!" The man pulled the dog back so Henry could sit up. Henry hugged the dog, its tail wagging so fast, it was a blur. "Fudgie." He buried his face in the dog's side.

"The others are waiting for you too."

"Fuji? Pepper? Ashes? Hero? And Sugar?"

"Them, too," said his grandfather. "You ready? Your grandmother is waiting to see you." The older man offered his hand to his grandson and helped him stand up.

"Thank you, miss, for helping me find my family again."

Henry took his grandfather's hand. The dog barked happily. He danced, leaped, and ran ahead as they vanished into the trees.

Autumn was happy Henry found the way back to his family. Was there anyone else here who needed her help?

She looked around the park. There were ghosts everywhere. Ladies in hoop skirts and parasols gossiped as they passed through a park bench. Men in waistcoats tipped their bowler hats when they met. People in military dress from the War of 1812 and both World Wars saluted soldiers who fought in the Gulf War and Afghanistan. They all walked among the living, each group ignoring the existence of the other. None were in distress.

Three women in long white cloaks stood on the path, watching her. She knew them from someplace. She pretended not to notice them, in case they disappeared. Once she got close enough, she stopped in front of them.

"Who are you, and why are you here?"

"Atropos, she can see us," the youngest of the three said. She looked to be a bit older than Autumn, but not much. She wore a T-shirt and jeans beneath her robe.

"I'm aware of that, Clotho," said the eldest woman. Her gray hair was in a bun on the top of her head. Wrinkles accented her emerald-green eyes.

The third woman looked to be in her midthirties and wore flowers in her hair. "She has the release potion in her hand, and there's an Earth stone in her pocket. There's still some of the oil from the stone on her hands as well." She smiled at Autumn. "And that's why you can see us. My name is Lachesis, this young woman is Clotho, and this is Atropos."

Autumn thought for a moment. "You're the Fates. Clotho gathers the souls from the Well of Time, Lachesis spins them into thread for the Tapestry of the Universe, and Atropos cuts the measure to mark the length of a person's life."

Clotho clapped her hands joyfully. "I knew you'd remember us!"

Atropos smiled. "What she means is, we met through your connection to Kali and Thanatos. You just see us so rarely; we're surprised you remember us."

Clotho leaned closer to Lachesis. "Is this about the knot?"

Lachesis nodded and put her fingers to her lips.

"Why are you here now?" Autumn asked, joining them as they walked the path toward the children's play area.

"Thanatos asked us to create the projections of Kali so you can help the *Ka*," Lachesis said.

"I was wondering how that worked." Autumn jumped out of the way of a bicycle, not realizing it was a ghost until it passed through a birdbath and kept going. "How much longer will I be seeing spirits this clearly?"

"Wipe the potion off your hand with this." Atropos gave Autumn a cloth with embroidery around the edges.

"What is it? Is it magical?"

"It's a handkerchief," Atropos said slowly. "You've heard the old rhyme, haven't you? 'One for blow and one for show'? Well, that's my show. It's perfectly clean."

Clotho rolled her eyes. "They might be a bit old-fashioned, but they work better on the potions than a plain paper tissue. But, if necessary, you can always use your sleeve or a pant leg."

"You can keep it. You might need it later."

Autumn wiped her hands, folded the hankie, and put it into her jacket pocket. She looked up to thank Atropos, but the three women were gone. No, not gone. Invisible.

"Curiouser and curiouser," she whispered. Autumn decided thinking about the Fates was just going to give her a headache of questions she couldn't find the answers to. The last thing she needed right now was more unanswered questions, so she decided to think about something easier, like her future existence. And that meant going to school.

Saint Katherine's Academy of the Arts, or Saint Kate's as it was known, was a specialty college that took students from elementary school all the way through to junior college. They taught all types of fine art, as well as decorative arts, performing arts, and crafts. She thought about what she could study. Could she draw? She'd put a sketch pad into her bag to try her hand while she was in the park. But maybe sculpture was more her thing? Her stepmother had made sure she knew how to sew, knit, and embroider. Was that a thing she could study? Fashion, or maybe costume design? Maybe she could take up weaving. Lachesis could always help her with her homework. She smiled at the absurdity of it. Maybe Kali was right. Maybe she was beyond the needs of a mortal school.

Autumn soon found herself in the children's play area. She wondered if she'd ever played in a park like this one. Somehow, she couldn't imagine her godmother pushing her on the swings. She remembered walking in a park with her father, but it seemed so long ago. Sometimes she couldn't remember his voice, but other times it was like he'd been there just a minute ago.

A child's *Ka* ran past. Autumn followed it, catching sight of it again as it flew down the slide. Autumn rounded the corner and watched the *Ka*'s host swinging on the monkey bars. The *Ka* turned cartwheels in the grass. The freckle-faced girl hung upside down by her knees. The image of Kali was by her shoulder. Autumn breathed a sigh of relief. The girl swung down. Kali was at the girl's feet. Autumn wasn't prepared to take a child and was deciding whether to run away when Kali's image jumped back up to the girl's shoulder.

The girl's *Ka* suggested something to the child, and the two began turning cartwheels and somersaults in the grass. During each flip, the image of Kali lagged behind by several seconds. The child finally stopped tumbling and ran to play on the swings. Autumn touched the Earth stone in her pocket and sauntered over to the swings. No sooner did Autumn find a swing close enough to touch the girl's hand than the child was off again. She was at the top of the monkey bars before Autumn could walk back across the sand. How was she going to touch the child? Autumn felt eyes boring a hole in the back of her skull. A woman stood beside the park bench, coffee in hand. Autumn wandered back toward where the woman waited.

"Is that your daughter?" The woman nodded. Autumn and the woman watched the child defy gravity. "I was just admiring your daughter's technique."

"She was in gymnastics for a long time. It's her first day out after being stuck at home with the flu."

The woman didn't seem worried and applauded when the child dismounted from the bars and climbed back up again. The modern world treated the flu as if it were no more than a bad cold, but Kali had taught her about the seriousness of it all. Autumn had learned all about different, dangerous strains of flu, from the Spanish Flu in 1919 to the Hong Kong Flu in the late 60s, and more recently, the H1N1.

The girl tumbled across the fading grass. The image of Kali had a devil of a time keeping up.

"Maybe you and your daughter can help me with something. I'm studying fashion design, and my dream is to be a costume designer. I have a project I'm working on for school."

Autumn pulled the sketch pad out of her purse. "We have to create outfits for an imaginary event. Some of my friends are designing gowns for galas or weddings, but I don't want to do what everyone else is doing. I was stuck for an idea, but your daughter may have saved me. She's inspired me to create costumes for a gymnastics troupe or something like that."

"You mean like Cirque du Soleil?"

"Exactly. Could I talk to your daughter?"

The mother stood up and called to her daughter. She skipped across the grass and stood beside her mother. The woman put her arm around her daughter's shoulder. "Simone, this is…"

"Autumn." She made sure she had some of the reattach potion on her palm before they shook hands. "I'm working on some costumes for a circus show. Can you help me?"

Simone bounced onto the bench. "Sure, what do you need?"

Autumn sat with Simone and her mother talking about costumes and sketching leotards, capes, and makeup. The girl was obsessed with sequins and glitter, fairies and unicorns, and swords and spears. Autumn made fast sketches of the outfit Simone described, much to the child's wonder. She watched Simone's *Ka* become healthier and the silver surrounding her more lustrous.

"Wow," Autumn said. "We've been sitting here for close to an hour. I've got to get home. More homework to tackle." Simone made a sour face, then smiled. Autumn did a fast sketch of Simone wearing the Warrior Princess helmet she'd described for the show's leading lady and gave it to her.

She'd have to find out about the delay. She promised herself to count to one hundred before she acted on a *Ka*, especially if the person was upside down.

Autumn waved goodbye and headed down the hill. She discovered she not only knew how to draw, but she wasn't half-bad either. Costume design seemed like a good career path. It also sounded so familiar.

She felt someone's eyes on her. She recognized the feeling of this particular spirit. All she would have to do was put some potion on her hand and find out who he was and why. It would be easy, but she couldn't bring herself to do it.

There was an empty park bench beside a huge bolder. She sat down. "Okay, Mr. Ghost. What do you want to show me?"

Autumn closed her eyes. She listened for the familiar whisper. She thought she heard it, but she wasn't sure. There was something there. It had to be a message from the ghost.

*utumn found herself standing in a small workroom. A calendar on the wall above a cutting table read June 1966. Rose threaded the sewing machine's needle and lowered the foot onto a cotton sleeve. Autumn could hear Rose's thoughts and knew everything that went on.

Rose was dating someone named Andy. He looked like her last boyfriend, Olivier, in a general way, but he didn't have Olivier's heart and spirit.

It was convenient. They worked in the same university theater group. He was the director. Rose made costumes. Their budget was so small, they had to go to every Salvation Army shop, used clothing store, and clothing factory that would donate fabric ends and damaged or returned clothes to look for material to rework into costumes for the productions. The machine whirred, drowning out the classical music coming from the transistor radio behind her.

The door burst open, and a young man ran into the room. He slammed the door and leaned against it. "You have to help me," he said breathlessly.

Rose snuck the large shears from the lower shelf of the machine's table and held them in her lap. The cast of the play had warned her about working in the theater by herself because junkies, with a reputation for robbing people, slept in the alley between the buildings.

Although, she didn't think she had anything to worry about with this person. His *Ka* seemed healthy enough. It just kept doubling over with laughter. It would wipe the tears from its eyes, seem to calm down, then slap its leg and start all over. Rose found it very hard to keep serious. It was easier if she didn't look at his *Ka*. She decided it best to focus on the stranger's square-jawed face and piercing eyes.

"I'm sorry, but I don't have any money. And I'm very busy, so could you please leave?"

"No, please. I'm the one who should apologize. I didn't mean to scare you. My name is Ed Sterling, I'm a part of the theater company." He bowed from the waist. "I'm an actor."

Rose stood up and placed the shears beside the sewing machine. Her deep curtsy made her feel as if she were greeting royalty, not some unknown actor. "My name is Autumn Rose Cassidy, but you may call me Rose."

"And you know how to sew?" Rose nodded. Eddie clapped his hands. "Excellent! Nice curtsy, by the way. Maybe you can teach it to Emma."

"I'm sure she'd prefer having a completed costume to learning to curtsy. So, if you'll excuse me..."

"Why bother with costumes? How does this sound? *The Twelfth Night—Naked!* It's sure to sell more tickets."

"But isn't the play about a woman who assumes the place of her twin brother?"

"Yeah?"

"If all the actors are naked, wouldn't that ruin her disguise?"

He sat down at the second sewing machine. "Good point."

"Now that's been settled, I'll get back to work." Rose checked the position of the sleeve, and with a light pressure on the sewing machine's foot peddle, the machine caught the fabric, sewing a perfect seam.

She could get the machine to control the length of the stitch and the tension of the thread. Automation was wonderful. She stopped the machine, snipped the threads, and placed the sleeve on the repurposed end table beside her. She pulled another piece of fabric from the laundry basket at her feet.

"You're really fast on that thing."

Rose jumped. "I thought you'd left."

"I still need your help."

"With what?"

Eddie stood up and turned around. His black trousers had split their seam from just below the waistband. Now she understood why the *Ka* was laughing. His partially exposed backside looked like a zebra, with his white underwear showing between his half-covered cheeks.

"I see."

"And all of Ville des Saintes will be able to see also. I'd run home to change, but I don't have a car. And I can't get on the bus like this. I'd be arrested." He fell to his knees, causing the fabric to tear loudly. "Please, can you help me? Can you fix my pants?"

"You'll have to take them off." Rose rolled her eyes at the way Ed wiggled his eyebrows and grinned. "The changing room is over there." She pointed to the back corner of the workroom. Rose handed him a bathrobe as he passed.

Ed pushed aside an old blanket and pulled the string to turn on the bare light bulb above his head. He stepped out a few moments later, wrapped in the old robe, his pants in his hand.

Rose took them and emptied the pockets onto the work table. She shook her head. "I'm afraid I can't help you. The fabric is too worn and weak to hold the seam anymore."

Eddie stood close to see what she was talking about. She showed him where the weave had started to fray and how easily the thread of the fabric came away as she brushed her fingers against the pants. Rose could feel his warmth through the bathrobe, against her bare arm. She stepped back and held the pants out to him, creating a black cotton shield between them.

"I'm sorry. You'd better go."

"I can't walk around Ville des Saintes like this. Someone will think I escaped from the hospital or something. Please, Ms. Cassidy. I need something to get me to my own front door."

She looked into his blue eyes. His expression and posture were so forlorn. Rose sighed. "What size pants do you wear?"

"Size thirty-four. Bless you, Ms. Cassidy." He waited patiently while she went through the costumes on the back racks. Most were donations, some had been used in previous plays. Some still had the tags with the actor's name and the play they'd appeared in like *Annie Get Your Gun* and *Oklahoma*. With all these cowboys on stage, there had to be a pair of jeans somewhere on the rack. She thought for a moment.

"Have you heard of a restaurant called *Lee's Gardens?*" Ed asked.

Metal hangers scraped against metal bars. "No, I'm sort of new in town."

"I thought so." He adjusted the bathrobe and sat down at the sewing machine. "Well, the restaurant. Lee's Gardens... nice place, and the food's good. I go there a lot."

Rose slowed her search. This might get awkward. After all, she and Andy were dating, although Andy was not someone who could commit to anything called a relationship. He was a bit too fond of the free-love movement.

"So, Ms. Cassidy, where are you from?"

"I'm British." Kali and Thanatos were so strict about relationships. She had worked very hard to show how trustworthy she could be, bringing another mortal into her life and still keeping her work a secret. She'd proven it to them by going out with Andy. Meeting a man and being together in public without a chaperone didn't mean an engagement; not like it did a hundred years ago.

"Your accent kind of gave it away. My parents were born in Ireland but came to Canada between the wars. Do you like Chinese food, Ms. Cassidy? Because Lee's Gardens has some of the best in the city."

If he asked her to dinner, she planned on saying yes. They would be two members of the same acting troupe sharing a meal.

Eddie stood up and looked over the racks. "I really appreciate you helping me like this."

They would have dinner. They would talk about the play and

about school. Completely innocent. She might even kiss him at the end of the evening.

Ed looked at his watch.

Rose found it. Buffalo Bill's costume from *Annie Get Your Gun*. The jacket was decked out with gold trim, medals, and huge buttons, but the pants were rescued from someone's black tuxedo. A little formal, but hardly noticeable.

"Did you find anything?"

"I might have." She checked the label inside the pants for the size. A bit big, but his belt or a couple of strategically placed safety pins should do the trick.

"Marvelous!" He checked his watch again. "I'll have just enough time to make it home and get ready for my date with Emma." Emma Whiting was the play's female lead and a 24-karat pain in the backside diva. So that was the kind of girl he preferred? The kind that would make him into a fool.

Rose walked out from between the racks and offered him a pair of patchwork pants in red, yellow, florals, and paisley. "I'm afraid these were the only pants in your size. They were worn by the fiddling clown in *Fiddler on the Roof*."

"Um... okay. There wasn't anything else?" Her look said it all. "Of course."

"If that's all. I'm very busy, and I would also like to get home to dinner."

"Thank you, Ms. Cassidy, for your time and your patience. I'll go change, and I'll get out of your hair."

He took the pants back to the changing room. Rose sat down at the sewing machine and pulled another piece of the costume she was working on from her work basket. She smoothed out the green cotton and pinned the pieces of the sleeve together. The radio announced a harpist playing a selection of Elizabethan folk music. The song *Greensleeves* came on first.

Rose started sewing, singing softly. Green sleeves, like the ones she was sewing. She wasn't being discourteous. He was the one who'd burst in on her. She removed some of the pins to better access the margin for the seam.

One of Ed's shoes slid to her side of the curtain. Rose looked at that poor innocent shoe, just a victim of chance and misadventure. She put her hands in her lap and shook her head. She couldn't do it.

"Wait a minute, Mr. Sterling."

Eddie stuck his head out from behind the curtain. "Did you call me?"

Rose got up and found his shoe. "I said, your shoe is out here." She handed it back to him. "I was also thinking about other costumes I'd seen on the racks, and I've thought of another pair of pants that might be more suitable. They're part of a suit, so you'll have to get them back here first thing tomorrow. The costume was very costly, and if the production company found I'd lent part of it out..."

"I swear to have them back first thing. Anything not to have to walk downtown looking like an ad for *Barnum and Bailey's*."

Rose went back into the racks and found the Buffalo Bill costume. Eddie looked worried when he saw the jacket, but relaxed when Rose presented him with a pair of black pants. Eddie was changed and back at her side in a flash. A gray Beatles T-shirt, high-top sneakers, and tuxedo pants were definitely a fashion statement.

He kissed her cheek. "Bless you, Ms. Cassidy. You're a lifesaver."

"And I'll have them back first thing tomorrow?"

"First thing. I promise."

"If you and those trousers are not back here tomorrow, I will track you down and follow you closer than your shadow at midday."

"Then maybe I won't bring them back."

"Excuse me?"

"Well, if it's a way to get to see you again and for us to spend some time together..." He shrugged.

"You could try asking me to join you for a cup of coffee."

"You're right. That's a much better idea. You wouldn't be angry because I had your trousers, and people wouldn't be staring when you yelled at me to take off my pants." Rose smirked. Eddie bowed with a dramatic flourish, worthy of a whole tuxedo. "Until tomorrow, Ms. Cassidy. And I'll even bring the coffee."

*utumn smiled as the memory ended. Rose had worked with *Ka* also. But better than that: costume design was in the family. It was also wonderful to know her grandmother had found love after her divorce. Rose and Eddie had been happy. "Thank you, Mister Ghost, for showing me that happiness, even if it wasn't mine."

*I*t may have been Thanksgiving, but there were no days off when you worked for the Goddess of Death. Autumn checked her watch and shivered as she waited for the bus.

Nora had invited her for a turkey dinner. She said she was using her Grandmother Sterling's recipe. Nora said Ava Sterling's dinners had always been delicious, and the hardest thing about her growing senile was her having to give up cooking and baking.

Rose had never learned to cook. Edward had tried to teach her. But she never really got beyond frying an egg. According to family lore, Rose's best skill in the kitchen was testing the smoke alarm.

Autumn couldn't remember if she had ever cooked a meal. Kali and Thanatos didn't need to eat. But someone must know their way around a kitchen because she'd eaten a hearty breakfast that morning. Maybe she'd ask her aunt to teach her how to cook.

Her aunt. Her aunt and her cousin. Thanksgiving dinner with her family. The whole thing made her smile.

Thanatos had dropped her off at the subway earlier. She'd planned to explore the town on public transport. Everything was on the weekend schedule. Somehow, she remembered all of the street names and most of the bus routes she needed to get around the city. She had crisscrossed the island working on her assignments from Kali and Thanatos, but it took a lot longer than she'd planned.

The few others in the line for the bus wore scarves, and some already donned gloves and hats. As the weather got colder, her work with the *Ka* would become more difficult. Once the snow came, everyone would add more layers of clothes. She'd be lucky to find a gap between a jacket cuff and a glove. She'd have to speak to Kali or the Fates about how to handle it.

Autumn stamped her feet to try to warm up, then looked up the street for the bus. She spotted Nora talking to another woman as they waited for the light to change. Autumn left the bus line to try to catch up to her.

This part of town was called the Rag District and it had been built up for the influx of European immigrants escaping the World Wars. Duplexes sat beside the clothing factories that had sprung up for new arrivals to work in. The children of those factory workers were Canadian-born and university-educated. Their parents encouraged them to find single-family homes in the suburbs. When the grandchildren of these immigrants came of age, they went searching for big rooms, high ceilings, and cheap rents. They flocked back to the Rag District's duplexes with their outdoor ironwork staircases and original plaster moldings, the same homes their parents and grandparents had worked hard to get away from.

Autumn turned the corner in time to see Nora go into a building that had once been a bank, the name still carved into the marble above the door. The sign in the window said it was now *The Akasha Yoga Studio*. She hadn't intended to follow Nora inside, but a cold rain had started to fall. Autumn went in to get out of the storm.

The exterior was granite and marble with Roman-style pillars. They had kept the stained-glass windows with their scenes of Canadian Industry: a steam engine passing through the Rockies; a tall ship, sails billowing, traveling over the horizon; a farm with a fruit-filled orchard and animals grazing around the barn.

The soft recessed lighting made the pale-yellow reception room more calming. Gray padded chairs stood between large wicker boxes filled with yoga mats. Shoes and boots were carefully placed in square cubes on the wall beside the coat rack.

Nora stood beside the door to another room chatting with a fellow student. She wore a T-shirt, with the album cover from *Meet The Beatles* on it, and tights. The other woman wore a color-coordinated outfit. A third woman joined them. She was much younger, with a butterfly tattoo on her shoulder and a gold stud in her belly button.

People left the classroom. Autumn took off her shoes and her jacket and followed Nora and her friends through the door.

"Can we help you with something?" the younger woman asked. Nora turned around.

"Autumn? What are you doing here?" She turned to her friends. "Amelia, Maggie, this is my niece."

Autumn couldn't think of what to say. She was too focused on the image of Kali floating beside Nora's knee.

"Autumn?"

"Sorry Aunt Nora. I was waiting for the bus, and I saw you cross the street. I thought we could get some lunch or something."

"I'll be taking the yoga class, and then I have to get home to start on the side dishes that go with our fabulous turkey".

"Taylor has been talking about nothing else," said Amelia. "She says your stuffing is to die for."

Not if Autumn had anything to do with it. This would not be Nora's last holiday. Autumn made a silent vow to her aunt, her cousin, and her… grandmother. Nora would see New Year's Eve. Autumn wasn't going to lose another family member. Not if she could help it.

Autumn tried to think of something to do. There had to be another way. She had to save Nora and protect Zoe. "Have you been doing yoga long?"

"A couple of years," Nora said. "I'm still pretty amateur."

"No way," said Maggie. "She's very good." Nora tried to shrug off the complement.

"No false modesty. I don't believe in it," Maggie said.

Amelia agreed. "Show your niece how good you are. Do the *Salamba Sirsana*. That's a type of headstand."

"Can you really do that?" Autumn asked. She remembered the little gymnast in the park.

"She doesn't need to see me hoist my butt into the air."

"But I want to," Autumn said. Maggie nodded. Autumn sat down on the floor to watch.

Nora stretched and moved into the pose. Autumn had the reattach potion on her fingertips. Nora clasped her hands together and placed them behind her head. Her forearms formed a triangle on the floor. Kali hadn't followed Nora's feet into the air. The Goddess was so close that Autumn could have kissed her.

Autumn brushed her fingers against Nora's elbow, so lightly she wasn't sure the ointment had worked, but the telltale warmth went up her arm. Nora's *Ka* began to normalize, laying on the mat beside Autumn.

"That's amazing!" Autumn said. More people entered the room. Nora righted herself. Autumn stood up. "I'd better go. It looks like you'll be starting soon."

"Dinner is at seven but come early if you want to hang out with Zoe and meet Amelia's daughter, Taylor," Nora said.

"Yes, right." Autumn waved when she got to the door. "I'll see you both later."

Autumn left the building and headed back to the bus stop. She didn't even mind the rain. Nora and Zoe were safe. Where was a rainbow when you needed one?

Zoe heard a key in the apartment's door. If her mother stayed true to form, she'd have her yoga shower, and nap until lunch.

"Zoe! I'm home!" Nora called as her shoes clattered against the wood floor. She leaned against the doorframe of her daughter's room. "I'm going to take a fast peek at the turkey, then jump into a shower. Did you baste the bird?"

Zoe stopped writing notes on her computer, but, keeping her eyes on the screen, she lifted her phone. "I've been true to the timer all morning."

"Perfecto, baby doll." She kissed her daughter loudly on the top of her head, then went back toward the kitchen singing *I Want to Hold Your Hand.*

Zoe stopped; her hands poised over the keyboard. She couldn't remember her mother ever singing unless there was already music playing. She closed the lid of her laptop and went to find Nora. Nora had taken the turkey out of the oven and danced as she basted.

"Mom? Are you okay? You took your pills this morning?"

"I feel wonderful. All the pills were taken." She wiggled her hips. "Hear the rattle?"

"But you're okay?"

"Perfect! Why?"

"I don't know. You seem different somehow."

"It must be the yoga. I had an amazing session today." She put the roasting pan back into the oven. "I feel so energized. If I hadn't driven Amelia to class, I would have walked home."

She closed the oven door with her foot. Holding the oven mitt like a puppet, she started to speak in a funny voice. "Well, Ms. Nora, you know what you have to do now?

"No, Mr. Plaid-face." Nora looked at the oven mitt. "What do I have to do?

"Well, Ms. Nora, I believe it may be time for your shower."

"Really Mr. Plaid-face?

"Indeed, Ms. Nora. You're a bit smelly, and not in a French perfume kind of way, either.

"Right you are, Mr. Plaid-face." She put the mitt down on the counter and patted it. She gave Zoe a big hug and left the room singing.

"Curiouser and curiouser," Zoe muttered. She shrugged and went back to her homework.

*Z*oe hung up the phone. She and Taylor were alone in the living room. The parental units were in the kitchen doing the last-minute preparations.

"Autumn's on her way up," Zoe said loudly

Taylor's father, Ethan, gave the thumbs-up sign. "Your mom's hands are full, so I was elected to give you the finger."

"Fah-ther!" Taylor fell back on the sofa. They could hear their mothers giggling as he went back to the kitchen. "Dad jokes."

"Better that than a joke for a Dad," Zoe said.

"He still hasn't called?"

"Not since I sent him a copy of his wife's email."

"I'm sorry."

Zoe stood up to answer the knock at the door. "On to important matters."

Autumn stood there holding a bunch of roses. She smiled as Zoe welcomed her in and introduced her to Taylor.

Nora came out of the kitchen carrying a turkey big enough for fifteen people. "Just in time."

Zoe took the flowers into the kitchen to put them into water. Taylor followed her to help bring out some other platters for the table.

"So now what do we do?" Taylor asked quietly.

"We be polite, and play nice, and eat." Taylor gave Zoe an odd look. "Tay, if we ruin this dinner party, my mom will be angry, your parents will be upset, and I'll be eating turkey leftovers for the rest of my natural life."

"All right. Shoulders back. Chin up. Smile pretty. It's showtime."

⁂

*T*he conversation stayed light over dinner. Nora's extra yoga energy turned her into a super-hostess. Zoe hoped there was a way to bottle it so she could save some for the holiday rush at the gallery. Her mom always looked so worn down during those weeks. And more often than not, New Year's Eve was spent in her pajamas in front of the TV and she'd be in bed by nine.

But tonight, she was a whirlwind on steroids. No glass stayed empty for very long, and she was passing food around even before anyone asked for something. Everything was delicious, and everyone was so full they couldn't even move away from the table to enjoy their coffee in the living room. Zoe, Taylor, and Autumn talked about some of the Halloween window displays they had seen downtown, each defending their favorite. Nora talked about the plans for the upcoming show and dropped some of the famous names of people who had RSVP'd. Amelia told some funny stories about the people she worked with at the Vale Hospital.

"So, Autumn," Ethan said as he passed the fruit platter. "Nora tells me you're going to register for Saint Katherine's tomorrow." Taylor let out a dramatic sigh. "Taylor, it's my job to get students settled into the school, and I love my job."

"I know Father. I was hoping to not talk about school this weekend."

"Oh well. We must all learn to live with disappointment." He turned back to Autumn. "Do you have an idea of what track you'd like to follow?"

"I've been thinking about it since Aunt Nora mentioned it. I think I'd like to go into costume design." Autumn thanked Amelia for the tray and passed it back to Nora.

"Do you have a portfolio?" Ethan asked.

"Nothing formal." Autumn took the napkin from her lap. "I can show you some of my drawings if you'd like." She got an 8 x 10 sketchbook from her shoulder bag and gave it to Ethan. Amelia and Taylor moved their chairs closer. Zoe and Nora stood up and walked around the table to look over Ethan's shoulder. Zoe looked over at Autumn. She sat in her chair, separate from everyone, hands folded in her lap, lips pressed together.

The first couple of pages were fast pencil sketches of the mall's interior. People were drawn as gestures more than in detail. There were some still-life drawings. The first few were of the leftovers from a meal and table settings. Ethan turned the page to a drawing of makeup and perfumes on a metal tray. Nora smiled at Zoe as she pointed out the mirrored tray from Rose's bedroom. The knot began to form in Zoe's stomach.

Zoe looked at her cousin. Her cousin was a real person, alone. The metal tray was just a tray. Zoe smiled. "It looks like art runs in the family. These are pretty good." Taylor nodded her agreement. Autumn smiled back, and Zoe noticed the tension leave Autumn's body as she relaxed back into the chair.

Ethan turned the page. There were drawings of a gymnast in some very odd costumes.

"Why is this unicorn wearing a Roman gladiator's helmet?" Taylor asked. "It looks like something someone from Cirque de Soleil would come up with after one too many at the company Christmas party."

Autumn laughed. "It kind of does. I was in the park on Snowy Hill and this kid flew around the monkey bars. Her mother was there, and I got to talking to her and the young acrobat. The little girl wanted to see what I was drawing, then she started feeding me costumes she would like to wear once she became famous. She was the one that sparked the idea of doing costume design. Not because she actually said anything. I watched her as she was tumbling and running around the park, and it all went from there. Those first few were costumes she suggested from her imaginary show." Autumn checked to see where they were in her book. "The next few are a bit more serious."

Ethan turned the page. Autumn had started adding colored-pencil to her drawings. The first was an elaborate drawing of a king in Elizabethan dress. On the following page was a fairy with large wings. She posed like a ballerina; her wand raised over her head. Her leg stretched out behind her as she stood *en pointe*.

"I don't think you'll have any problem getting into the program," Zoe said. Taylor and Nora agreed emphatically.

"I think you may be right, Zoe." Ethan closed the sketchbook and brought it around the table to return it to Autumn. "Welcome to Saint Kate's."

Zoe noticed tears in her cousin's eyes.

Autumn's room looked like a hurricane had gone through. Another shirt she tried on and discarded was added to the high pile on the bed. She didn't believe she had ever been one of those people who could stare at a closet filled with clothes and moan because she had nothing to wear. She wanted to make a good impression. She wanted to look sharp and artistic, but not like a wannabe hipster who was trying too hard to look sharp and artistic. The whole thing was maddening. Is that what high school does to a person?

Maybe Kali was right. Homeschooling might be her best bet, especially with her wonky memory. Would she remember how to deal with all the technology Zoe used? Could she remember any of the books she'd read? What about math? What if she couldn't remember the multiplication table, let alone formulas for geometry or algebra?

She pulled on a long-sleeved gray T-shirt. It matched one of the shades in her herringbone leggings. Autumn pulled a pair of small silver hoop earrings from her jewelry box and sat in front of the mirror to put them on. What if her memory prevented her from learning anything? What if she sat in class, got tons of great information on fascinating topics, but forgot it all by the next day? What if nothing stuck?

There was a knock at her bedroom door. "*Koukla mou*, I have it," Thanatos said. Autumn opened the door, and he handed her a brown envelope. "Your school marks from before."

"Thank you, Uncle Theo." The envelope had her name on it and a logo she didn't recognize. The document in the envelope had her grades, but the date was smudged and illegible.

She'd been in a high school, but she had no idea where it was or if she had friends while she was there. Was there someone from her old life wondering why she never called? "I've been thinking. Maybe Kali was right. I should wait and start school next year."

"No. That's not a good idea at all." He shook his head. "Not even a little bit. Autumn, you live with Death. You work with Death. You need to know what it means to be alive. Meet people. Tell jokes. Laugh sometimes."

"But we have fun. Don't we?"

"We have fun, *Koukla*, but it's not the same thing. I wish you could remember Rose. Rose worked very hard for Kali—so hard and so long, I was afraid she was forgetting how to be human. She argued about not wanting to go into the world too—before she went out and learned to be part of it. She felt pain. And had a few problems. But for all of her nervousness, I don't think she would trade a million years of safety behind these walls for one minute of the love she shared with Eddie, or Nora, or Zoe. I would wish that type of memory for you, Autumn."

"Uncle Theo, if you and Kali have been with me, how were you living with Rose, too?"

"We are gods, *Koukla*. I'm here with you now, but I'm also with soldiers fighting in the Middle East, I'm talking to a young man with cancer in Australia, and I'm holding a woman's hand in a hospital in Saskatchewan. I feel and see all of them, all at the same time." He crossed his arms. "So, Autumn Rose Cassidy, am I driving you to school?

"It won't be necessary." She smirked at his scowl. "Aunt Nora is coming to pick me up."

"Bravo, *Koukla mou!*" He kissed her on the forehead.

"Uncle Theo," Autumn said as he headed out the bedroom door, "are you telling me the secret to life is doing my homework?"

"It always has been." He tapped the door frame. "It always has been, and it always will be."

*N*ora parked in the visitor's lot, and then she, Zoe, Taylor, and Autumn all walked across the street to Saint Katherine's. Autumn looked up at the school and released the breath she didn't realize she'd been holding. The building had once been a convent affiliated with the church next door. There was a French language college on the other side of the church.

Zoe pointed to the circular building behind one of the more modern wings of the school. "That's the building everyone in the school drools over. It might not look like much, but it houses the Captain's Theater, named for the actor who played Captain Church on the TV series *Star Harbor*, who graduated from the school, and the Sterling Art Gallery, named for my grandparents." Autumn nodded. She would have a lot to live up to.

There were a few stairs to get into the main part of the building, the oldest part of the school, made of fieldstone. A large stained-glass window shone above the door. She'd seen this building before. She remembered how the jeweled colors from the circular window reflected on the white marble floor.

She thought about the different corridors, the nuns moving silently from one place to another. She remembered the chapel and the scent of beeswax candles and their light on the polished wooden pews.

When they walked through the door, except for the reflections from the window, it was all different. White walls appeared where no wall had been, separating the hallway into sections and rooms. Display cases hung where religious symbols had been. The wooden paneling was replaced with drywall. Even though it was early, students moved through the hallways, carrying big portfolios, tool-boxes, and mysterious long black tubes.

Nora kissed her daughter and wished her and Taylor a good day. Zoe and Taylor waved goodbye and went down a short staircase toward their lockers. Nora led Autumn down another hallway toward the administration offices.

There were hallways and doorways leading off the circular entry-way. Autumn prayed her memory would hold long enough for her to locate her classrooms.

They turned a corner and saw Taylor's father talking to a tall Black woman. Autumn recognized her, but couldn't place her.

"Good morning, Ethan," Nora said.

"Hello, Nora, Autumn. This is Ms. Oya Bridges. She's teaching Special Projects this semester."

Oya smiled. "It's lovely to meet you both." She tilted her head. "Are you Autumn Rose Cassidy?" When Autumn nodded, she clapped her hands. "Storms and stars; I thought so. I won't be offended if you don't recognize me. I helped care for you when you were very young, when your father worked in Jamaica for a while. You favor his mother."

"You knew my Grandmother Rose?"

Oya paused. "I met her when I came to Canada. I didn't even realize the connection until recently."

Ethan held open his office door. "Shall we, ladies?"

"Mr. Main," Ms. Bridges said. "If Ms. Cassidy qualifies, I would welcome her in my workshop."

"Zoe and Taylor are in that class, too," said Nora.

"I'm sure you'll learn a lot," Ms. Bridges said. "Especially when it means working with your family."

Autumn nodded. "I think I'd enjoy that."

Ethan smiled. "One down, seven more classes to go."

*A*utumn made it through her first class, with one more to go before lunch. She was getting tired of this game of *Where's the Classroom*. Sometimes the numbers followed a logical pattern and were easy to find. But other times, well, there should be another way for the administration to show they were as creative as their students. Abstract models should never be used in interior design.

Autumn checked her schedule and the map of the school in her agenda. The sign said the building for her art history class was supposed to be here.

"You look like you could use a little help."

Autumn looked up. A blond boy with light blue eyes stood in front of her.

"I'm looking for C-309."

"We're in the 'C' building. You came in through that doorway there. Three-oh-nine, however, is one of the hidden classrooms. Follow me. I'm heading there too." He started walking. She shoved her agenda into her shoulder bag and rushed to catch up. He slowed a bit. "My name is Jake Kempt, by the way."

"I'm Autumn Cassidy. A pleasure to meet you."

"First day?" Autumn nodded. Jake opened his arms, like a gameshow presenter showing the winning prizes. "Well then, Autumn, allow me to welcome you to Saint Kate's, home to artists, actors, weirdos, and whack-a-doodles."

Autumn grinned. "And which department are you in?"

"I'm a 24-karat whack-a-doodle." He smirked. "I'm in the jewelry and metals department. My brother is in wood and furniture design."

"You two must have interesting arguments."

"Why do you say that?"

"Well, a millimeter for a woodworker is considered really tiny, but for a jeweler, it's huge."

"I never thought of it that way. Mostly we argue over brother stuff and over hammers and sandpaper." Jake opened the classroom door. "Milady."

"Why thank you, good sir."

utumn dragged herself up the stairs to her bedroom. It wasn't that she wasn't used to getting up early. And she knew it wasn't because she had to sit in class and listen to the teachers. Maybe it was trying to get her mind to take in all the new information. Or maybe it was having to encounter an endless stream of humanity.

She was exhausted. Her bed was there in the middle of her room. Her beautiful, comfortable bed. She flopped face down onto it without even taking off her shoes.

"What are you doing *Beti?*" Kali came out of Autumn's closet carrying some wire hangers and clear dry-cleaner bags.

"Hello Auntie-ji," she mumbled into the pillow. "It's been a long day."

"Was school a success?"

"Yes. But I think I wore out my brain. I'm off to take a little nap until dinner."

"Except you and Thanatos have work to do."

Autumn picked up her head. "But I have homework to do."

"Autumn, you agreed to continue working with me, if I agreed to let you go to school. Well, you're in school. So now you have to work with me." She picked up Autumn's coat and purse and put them within easy reach.

Autumn shrugged into the sleeves and sighed when Kali offered her the jewelry box. She found her grandmother's locket and put it on. The two stones were on her dresser. She put one into each of her coat pockets.

"Where am I going today?"

"The Guilbault Library. Those who watch for such things tell of a spirit haunting the shelves." Kali turned to leave. "Go and help them. Your dinner will be ready when you get home."

Autumn was about to follow her. "Might as well kill two birds, as they say." She grabbed her knapsack with her homework in it and ran down the stairs to meet Thanatos.

# OCTOBER 10TH, 2017

Zoe pulled Taylor toward the classroom. Taylor groaned, "I hate these early classes."

"Yes dear. Now be a good girl and drink your coffee."

"It's too hot," she whined. "Can't I get a medical excuse to skip this class?"

"What medical excuse?"

"I'm allergic to morning." Taylor shuffled through the hallway.

"Okay. Let's go talk to your father about it."

Taylor harrumphed as she sat down at her desk. "Zo-wee, you are so mean."

"Yes dear. Drink your coffee. You'll feel better." Zoe pulled out the binder with the notes she'd taken for their installation. "I was thinking about some of the materials we could use. What do you think of this list? Taylor. You have to open your eyes if you want to read the list."

"You're making me work too hard." Taylor leaned on her elbow and looked at the binder.

Joshua and Jacob entered the room, sitting at the desks in front of Zoe and Taylor. They turned in unison.

"Good morning ladies," said Jake. "How goes your project?"

"Considering we only started last week? Perfectly," said Taylor.

"What are you two working on? Did you find any famous dog walkers in your travels?"

"We found the stars and the director of a silent film called *Those Bohemian Sisters of Mine*," Josh said. "Marnie is going to be working with us. She has some excellent ideas. She's in the film department, you know, knows a lot about classic films."

He was always trying to get under Taylor's skin, but she wasn't going to bite. Taylor smiled and said, "Just don't leave her to do all of the work."

"Zoe," Jake said. "Have you met the new girl, Autumn Cassidy?"

"Yes. Why?"

"What do you know about her? Like, is she seeing anyone or anything?"

Zoe shrugged her shoulders and went back to her notes. "Excuse us. We have work to do." She pushed the binder toward Taylor and pointed to a word on the page. Taylor doodled a figure of a hanged man with Xs over his eyes. An arrow pointed to the figure, and she wrote "Jerk!" beside the arrow. Zoe smiled. "That's a great suggestion."

Oya Bridges walked into class, followed by Autumn. "Can we please get these desks into a circle? We have a lot to discuss and much to share today." She turned. "Autumn, why not take a seat beside Zoe over there? Zoe Williams, please wave so our newest student can find you."

Autumn moved a desk into position. Jake moved his desk beside hers. "Hi again," he said. "Weird we're both here too. That means we have four classes together. It must be fate."

"Or bad luck," Zoe muttered. Autumn smirked and looked sidelong at her cousin.

"Have you had a chance to see the outline for the project?" He pulled it from his binder and leaned in close, so they could read it together. "If you like, we still have an opening in our group. We're doing it on some film stars from the silent film era of the 1920s."

"I hadn't thought about it yet. I mean, this is the first time I'm reading this paper," Autumn said. "There are a lot of people buried in Snowy Hill."

"We could take a walk around there on Saturday, go to get a bite to eat. Maybe catch a movie or something?"

Zoe's head came up. She looked over at Autumn and held her breath. He knew she was sitting right here. If Autumn took her ex too, it would be the *perfect* school year.

"Or you could come and join our group," Taylor said. "Right Zoe?"

Zoe nodded. "Yeah. Of course."

Jake was such a jackass. The only reason he gave for them not seeing each other was his brother broke up with her best friend. But it's perfectly okay to ask her cousin out? She wished he would join the silent era and shut up forever. His lips exuded bovine excrement!

"I mean, Rose was your grandmother too. Right? Think of all the stuff you'll find out about her." Zoe leaned over to talk to Jake. "Autumn and I are first cousins."

"But our group is going to be way more fun."

Oya stood in front of them. "I see you're settling in, but you don't have to decide what project you intend to work on this very moment. Give yourself time to think about it."

Autumn nodded. "Thank you, Ms. Bridges, but if it's okay with you, I'd like to work with Zoe and Taylor on the Sterlings." Oya agreed and continued around the class to see what people worked on.

"What about our date?" Jake asked.

"If walking through a cemetery is your idea of a great first date, then no thank you," Autumn said as she leaned toward Zoe and Taylor. "Do I have a lot to catch up on?"

"All right, ladies and gentlemen," Oya called from the center of the circle. "Please take out your notebooks and planners. Time to learn how to create your production schedule. By the end of the hour, you will have divided up the research tasks and set up some team meetings. And, if you are fortunate, you might even have an idea for your installation's design and a possible list of materials. I know it's a tall order, but I have faith in your abilities."

*S*o many classes, so much homework. Zoe sighed as she made another note in her agenda. The day seemed to be getting away from her. The easels were set up in a circle around a central platform. Zoe opened her large portfolio, pulled out a stack of newsprint, and clipped it to the easel's board. Joshua took his place near her and Taylor. He tried to start a conversation, but she pointed to her earbuds and shrugged her shoulders.

Her phone wasn't playing any music. The thing wasn't even turned on. She used this tactic to keep people from bothering her when she wanted to think. She and Taylor were going to the library after class to start the research for their big art project. Once they found the theme they wanted to go with, they could begin planning the artwork. Autumn wouldn't be meeting them because she was meeting with some of her teachers to get makeup assignments.

Taylor came into the class and set up her station between Zoe and Joshua. She waved at Zoe, sat down on her stool, and closed her eyes. Zoe took her headset off, put everything into her bag, and did the same. It was a trick they had learned from Grandpa Eddie, a way of leaving all disruptive thoughts and anything else that could interrupt their artistic flow outside the classroom door.

She heard more people come in. The scraping of stools. The rustle of paper. The hushed whisper as students caught up on the doings of the day. Zoe heard Joshua talking to his brother, or he could have been talking to himself. Their voices were almost identical.

"Thank you, but I've worked with an easel before." Zoe opened one eye. Jacob was helping Autumn set up between Joshua's station and his.

It wasn't like her cousin was stalking her or anything. As soon as Zoe knew Autumn would be coming to Saint Kate's, she should have realized they would end up in a few classes together. Drawing Methods and Techniques was one of the core courses all students had to take, along with English, French, math, and Canadian history.

Zoe tapped Taylor on the knee. When she opened her eyes, Zoe nodded toward Autumn and the twins.

"Should we rescue her?" Taylor whispered.

Zoe thought for a moment. "Not yet."

Ms. Masters walked into the classroom followed by a tall twentysomething man with shoulder-length hair. She spoke to him for a few minutes as she polished her glasses on the tail of the oversized men's shirt she wore as a smock. He nodded and headed toward what Zoe thought was the storage closet. Ms. Masters was one of Zoe's favorite teachers. She looked so relaxed, but when she started talking about art, she became very animated. It was like paint and ink ran through her veins. All of her cells ran on sculpture dust. She could talk about something as weird as a concrete brick, and suddenly it became wondrous and beautiful, made only of shadows and light.

Autumn brought Ms. Masters some papers. She read them as she adjusted the clip in her long brown hair. Ms. Masters said something Zoe couldn't hear and put them into her briefcase. Autumn smiled and waved at Zoe as she made her way back to her easel.

"Everyone!" Ms. Masters said. "Five more minutes to set up and get the socializing out of your system."

"How's your day going, Autumn?" Taylor asked.

"Wonderfully overwhelming. I just hope I can catch up with everything."

"You will," Zoe said. "It's not like you have a choice."

"And if you need any help, I'm always available," Jake said with a smile. "Day or night. Let's exchange cell numbers, so we can keep in touch."

Autumn smiled at him. "Thank you for the offer, but my cell number is restricted. You understand."

Zoe smirked. She could feel the chill radiating off her cousin. Her grandmother was able to do the exact same thing. It might have been being raised in a military family or trying to sell art to people who believed their privileged lifestyle gave them a pass on etiquette, but Rose could tell someone to get lost, and they would thank her for it. Autumn could get that same tone in her voice. God, Zoe hoped it was genetic.

Ms. Masters clapped her hands. "Stations people. It's time to draw."

The class settled down. "Today, we're going to start working with a live model. Can someone please knock on the changing room door?" The door opened, and the young man came out wearing a short kimono and carrying a pole. His legs and his feet were bare. "Donn, whenever you're ready." He nodded and stepped up on the platform. "All right people. Charcoal at the ready. We're going to start with some quick gesture poses." She spoke to the model. "Three minutes each?"

"That's fine," Donn said. His voice was deep, with a bit of an Irish brogue. "But if you could please signal when the time comes to change, that would be delightful."

"Of course. Whenever you're ready."

Donn removed his robe and let it fall to the ground.

He was naked. Completely and utterly without a stitch of anything.

Zoe swallowed hard. She and Taylor looked at each other. They looked back at the naked man. Zoe looked at the other people in the class. Everyone seemed to be in shock. The twins had stepped away from their easels and were whispering together behind Autumn's back. She seemed to be the only one drawing.

"Come on people. He's only going to hold this pose for three minutes. Draw."

Zoe looked at the man. He was still naked but leaning against the pole like he was using it to move a raft. The pole was quite long. No! Not long. Stop thinking. Just draw. But he still wasn't wearing any clothes. And Taylor was no help, with that stupid smirk on her face. It was the same look she got when she read her mom's spicier romance novels. What was Zoe going to do? This building had been a convent, for God's sake.

The model had his back to her for the next few poses. People's backs were safe. She could draw people's backs, as long as she didn't look too far down. Oh God! She looked! She cursed her Celtic heritage that left her fair-skinned and red-headed. She could feel the blush creeping up to her hairline.

Zoe looked at the other students. They drew, but they weren't as animated as when they drew fruit or those huge Styrofoam shapes. Taylor drew, focused on her paper, rarely looking up at the model. She chewed on her lips, definitely not her usual Taylor self. OMG, was Zoe looking at him too often?

How was she going to do this type of thing for homework? What would her mother say when she saw her sketchbook filled with naked men?

Ms. Masters clapped her hands. "And time for a break! We resume in three minutes with longer poses."

"If they wanted the poses to be longer, they should have chosen a different model," Josh muttered to his brother. He started to sing *Brown Chicken Brown Cow*. His brother elbowed him in the ribs.

Zoe rolled her eyes. She felt a hand brush her shoulder, just like her grandmother used to do when she had a secret to tell her. "Think of the human body as a bunch of shapes," said the voice in her ear. Zoe nodded. Rose was sending her a message from beyond. She peeked toward the sound of the voice, expecting to see Rose's ghost.

It was Autumn. "You'll feel less self-conscious if you see the model as a series of ovals and lines. It's how I get through it."

"You've done life drawing before?"

Autumn paused. "I have, or I think I must have."

Zoe was about to speak when Ms. Masters clapped her hands to resume class. Autumn went back to her station. Zoe leaned over to Taylor and shared Autumn's advice. They closed their eyes to refocus themselves and took a deep breath. Zoe saw the model with fresh eyes. She looked over at Autumn and smiled. Autumn winked back.

It was as if Autumn had removed a film from her eyes or cast some kind of spell. Zoe began to draw with abandon. Every line had strength and purpose. She stepped back from the easel, not believing she looked at her own work.

"Very nice," said Ms. Masters, before she continued around the circle.

he building Zoe and Taylor lived in came into view when Uncle Theo turned the corner. He pulled up in front of their door.

"All right team," said Zoe. "Tomorrow, we meet at the library during our study period.".

"I'm afraid I can't," said Autumn. "I have a makeup test in French class, and it's going to be taking place during study period."

"Okaaaaay." Zoe thought for a moment. "Will you have time to start sorting through the stuff in the attic at Rowan House? Grandma Rose had a bunch of the gallery's photo albums and some scrapbooks with newspaper clippings and stuff. Some of it is at the gallery. I'll talk to my mom about getting into the storerooms there. But I'm sure there's a wealth of stuff at Rowan House, and if the albums ended up any where, it would be in the attic."

"They shouldn't be too hard to find," Autumn said.

"Except we're talking about *the attic*," Zoe said. "That was Grandpa Eddie's domain. His filing system was, how shall we say... unique."

"That bad?" Taylor asked.

"As Grandma Rose used to say, it was like the Bermuda Triangle barfed up there. Or she would say Grandpa was organizationally challenged, depending on her mood."

"Okay," said Autumn. "I'll start there tonight after I study for the test."

"And Zoe and I will be at the library seeing what we can come up with."

"We can meet at Rowan House on Saturday and compare notes and go through what I find," Autumn said.

"Sounds like we've got a plan," Zoe said before she and Taylor exited the car.

Autumn sat in a deep window well, her shoulder to the glass. There was a graveyard behind the church next door. Autumn stared at the tombstones, ignoring the French book balanced on her raised knees. The day was so overcast, it was hard to tell where the sky ended, and the Earth began. The cemetery held many of the soldiers who had returned from the war with the Spanish Flu, and the sisters and medical staff who had treated them and fell ill as well.

People walked by on their way to class, sometimes alone, sometimes in small groups. Autumn watched their ghostly reflections in the window.

"Storms and stars, child. There's more information in the book than in the graveyard." Oya Bridges stood beside her. "Mind if I join you?" Autumn closed the book and made space for her teacher to sit down. "How are you finding your classes?"

"They're okay, I guess."

Oya narrowed her eyes. "That isn't what you wanted to say, is it?"

Autumn looked down and hoped she wasn't blushing.

"Okay, I will ask you again, but be honest this time. How are you finding your classes?"

"Most times, with a really good map."

Oya laughed. "See? That didn't hurt a bit."

Autumn smiled. "I was going to send you an email later today. It's about the installation." Autumn took a deep breath. "I don't think I should stay in the class." She wanted to mention her wonky memory but thought otherwise. "This is my first year here. The others have been studying here for years. Getting into this school is competitive, and getting into this workshop is something gifted to the most creative. I feel like I cut the line because my grandmother was a supporter of the school. Like I got in because of my bloodline and not because of what I can do. Am I making sense?"

The wind hit the window, shaking the glass.

"Perfect sense. But I am like a gatekeeper. Do you think I would have suggested you joining my class if I didn't feel you would prosper from it? Rose was a lovely woman who never acknowledged her own talents or her own potential. She was always helping other people and forgetting things that would satisfy her in her own life."

Autumn thought about the work she did for Kali and how long Rose had done the same thing. "What if that was what Rose wanted? What if she wanted to fade into the background?"

"Storms and stars, Autumn. A person can be in the background without making themselves invisible. She should have known that. She should have been taught that." Oya sighed. "She came from a generation that put their husbands first. So her life became about supporting the gallery and helping build The Crayon Box Collective. That was important work, and I'm not making light of it one little bit. But Edward Sterling was larger than life. I brought you into the workshop hoping you would join with Zoe to bring Rose out of the shadows. She deserves to be remembered. I want you to discover who Rose truly is. What her art is like. What made her into the woman she became."

Autumn stood up. "I guess I'll get this French test out of the way so I can get to work on our installation."

"Good girl. I'll let you get back to your studies. See you in class."

"Thank you, Ms. Bridges."

"Please, call me Oya. I prefer the informality."

oe and Taylor stared intently at the computer screen.

"How's it going?" a voice asked suddenly.

Zoe gripped the edge of the desk to keep from jumping out of her skin. Taylor pressed her hands to her chest. Oya apologized, promising to make as much noise as the school library would allow, next time.

"We decided to start with a general internet search first," Taylor said. She was taking notes of possible leads and ideas for artwork. Zoe sat at the keyboard.

"There's a lot of information on my grandfather and The Crayon Box Collective."

Oya nodded. "Storms and stars, but I remember reading about the fallout when their name started making the newspapers. It was a very daring idea for its time, you know. In 1973, when the group started, things were still pretty chaotic. The Vietnam War was still going on, and there were all these protests against it, you know. Civil rights and women's rights were still in their infancy and being fought for. Same-sex relations had been decriminalized in 1969, but police raids were still going on. The Crayon Box Collective was seen as an act of revolution."

She looked from one girl to the other. "Creating a group of artists which welcomed everyone—women, minorities, and different sexual preferences—was unheard of. It shook the old establishment more than they would ever admit, then or now."

Zoe nodded. "Grandpa Eddie had friends who were part of the Computer Lab Protests at McCord."

"What protests?" Taylor asked.

"Some students charged a professor with racism." Zoe leaned back in her chair. "They took their complaints to the dean, but the whole thing was swept away. The board never even spoke to the students or the professor. The students had a sit-in at the school's computer lab, and the police were called in. It was a mess. Sally Jennings, one of The Crayon Box Collective, was arrested. Her mugshot became part of the painting that hangs in McCord University's library building."

"Sally Jennings's painting?" Taylor asked. "Is that what it's about?"

Oya smiled. *"Obtuse Angles for the Overeducated.* One of the first works publicized under The Crayon Box banner."

"Between The Crayon Box Collective, Sterling's Fine Art and Whatnot, and his charity work, I could probably create a whole book about Edward Sterling," Zoe said. "A really, really thick book." She thought back to last summer's reading list. "Like *Don Quixote*-on-steroids thick."

"Continued-in-next-backpack thick?" Taylor asked. "Or is it more add-a-plank-of-wood-and-you-can-bungee-jump thick?"

"Both." Zoe giggled, then quickly covered her mouth before they got shushed.

"And your grandmother's book?" Oya asked. "How thick would that one be?"

"So far, we can hold it together with a single staple." Taylor sighed.

"There doesn't seem to be much about her or her work at the gallery, or anything else." Zoe sounded dejected. "Most of what we've found just mentions her as my grandfather's wife."

Oya pulled up an extra chair. "Have you tried doing any searches using her maiden name?"

Zoe thought for a moment. "I don't know what that is." She looked surprised. "Even the footstone on her grave has her married name on it."

"What about your cousin?" said Taylor. "Maybe she knows something."

"Why not try your cousin's family name?" Oya said. "It may bring you to that branch of the family tree through the back door. There's probably a lot to discover there."

Zoe typed "Autumn Rose Cassidy" into the search engine. There was a much longer list than she expected. The first few listings were articles about her grandmother's work as a textile artist. She clicked open a couple of the images. "It says she was one of the founding members of the collective too." Zoe studied a magnificent tapestry of a woman and a tiger.

Taylor leaned over her shoulder to read the caption. "*Mothers Meet*, woven silk, wool, and hand-dyed cotton. Embroidered with glass beads and gold and silver thread. Photograph courtesy of the National Gallery of Ottawa. What the fu—" Taylor caught Oya's eye. "Ford hatchback?"

"My grandmother never said anything." She clicked open pictures of tapestries and quilts held in galleries, museums, and private collections all over the world. "My mother never said anything." Zoe could feel the tears gathering. "Why wasn't I ever told my grandmother was such a celebrated artist?"

Zoe tried another link. It was an old yearbook from Baron Crosby High School. It was one of the older schools in Ville des Saintes, and it had educated many famous authors, actors, politicians, and lawyers whose parents had come to Canada as immigrants around the time of the First World War. There was her grandmother's yearbook picture. Both she and her mom had a strong resemblance to her Grandma Rose, but Autumn could have been her clone.

"What was Rose's quote?" Taylor asked. "I saw my mom's. It was something about truth and beauty. It was pretty lame."

Zoe enlarged the page. "It's by Mary Shelley, the woman who wrote *Frankenstein*. 'Life and death appeared to me ideal bounds, which I should first break through, and pour a torrent of light into our dark world'."

Taylor leaned back in her chair. "Rose was emo."

"There are a lot more links to research." Zoe scrolled down the page. "There's even an Autumn Rose Cassidy listed on a passenger manifest from the 1800s."

"That's amazing," Oya said. The bell rang, and the girls gathered their books for their next class. "It looks like the roots of your family tree run fairly deep." Oya turned to leave. "Good luck with your search."

"Thanks." Taylor waited until Oya was out of earshot. "1800s? Please. I don't think Grandma Rose was that old."

Zoe put her backpack on. "Her artwork was amazing! I wonder why my grandparents never talked about it?" She sighed. It seems there was more to Grandma Rose than anyone had cared to share.

Zoe peeked into Sterling's Fine Art and Whatnot's executive office. Nora's upcoming appointments and reminders were written on an old blackboard behind what used to be, Eddie's desk. It was one of Zoe's favorite finds, rescued from Baron Crosby High School during their renovation from a school to a community outreach center. Her grandfather's initials were carved into the pine wood frame. (Although he claimed it was a coincidence and never actually confessed to putting them there.)

Zoe strolled into the room and waited for her mother to finish writing in her notebook.

"Hi baby doll. How was school?"

"It's still there. Mom? Did I tell you about the installation we're working on for my Special Projects class?"

"Does it have to do with you going to the cemetery a few weeks ago?"

Zoe nodded. "Taylor, Autumn, and I have to create some artwork describing a person's life experience. We were given special permission to do ours on Grandpa Eddie and Grandma Rose."

"Do you need some money for art supplies?"

"Yes, but not yet. We're still doing research." Zoe sat in the chair opposite the desk. "We've found lots of information on Grandpa, but finding anything about Grandma seems to be close to impossible. Everything we've found is about her being a Sterling."

"I see." Nora closed the cap on her pen. "Maybe you should just work on something for Grandpa. I have his clippings book here somewhere."

"We can't. My teacher says it has to be about both of them, and this is going to count for a big chunk of my grade." Zoe leaned forward. "Mom, did you know Rose was a textile artist?"

"I did. She worked under her maiden name, Rose Cassidy." Nora started searching the shelves in her office. "But if it's Autumn's last name too, I guess it wasn't her maiden name. It was the name of her first husband. I wonder what her maiden name really was?" Nora had a strange look on her face as she took a book off the shelf. It was a large coffee table book: *Not Your Granny's Quilt: Textile Art of the 20th Century.*

Nora put the book on her desk. It fell open to a page that had been looked at many times. She put the book in front of her daughter. Zoe saw one of the tapestries she'd seen on the computer. A second tapestry had the image of a bird raising itself from the blue and red flames of a fire. She turned the page. There was a photo spanning the full width of the book. It was a set of three wall hangings.

The collection was called *The Tarot Reading*. The first image was of a woman in a gold sari pouring stars into the ocean. The sky behind her was dark, filled with gray clouds. The earth beneath her bare feet was blood red. The second showed a man in a hooded cloak riding a white horse across a barren field. The sky was white with smoke and fire. The last was of a Black woman dancing in a lightning storm. A plantation house in the background was engulfed in flames. Flashes of gold and orange jumped from her hands. Tropical leaves decorated the edges of the tapestry. Men and women dressed in white looked no bigger than dolls as they crawled toward the central figure.

"Now there's a cheery piece—not."

"I think those were the last pieces my mother ever created."

"Why did she stop?"

"Eddie's father died not long after I was born. My father tried to get his mother to move into Rowan House, but she refused. Grandma Ava started to develop memory problems not long after that, and Rose ended up on-call. Eventually, Rose hired a woman to help out... What was her name? She was named after a Voodoo Goddess." Nora smiled. "Oya... but I can't remember her last name. She was a miracle worker. She stayed with my grandmother until she passed away."

Like her teacher's name? "What do you remember about the caregiver?"

"She was quite a striking woman if I remember correctly. Tall, mahogany skin. And she wore her hair in long, thin braids, which she kept piled on her head."

"You wouldn't happen to know if we have a photo of her?" Zoe wanted to take the words back as soon as she'd said them.

"There might be some from Ava's ninetieth birthday party, but they'd be at Rowan House."

It had to be a coincidence. There was no way her young art teacher could have been her great-grandmother's caregiver. *Wait. What?*

"All the family photos are still at Rowan House? You didn't bring any of them home?"

"I thought we'd be moving there, and..."

"Oh great!" Zoe scowled and leaned back in her chair. A virtual stranger was the keeper of her baby pictures. When had everything become so complicated?

Nora leaned against the desk. "I thought you and Autumn were getting along."

"Part of me wants to like her, but part of me is still pissed off. Why should she be able to waltz in from Never-Never Land and be handed everything on a silver platter?"

"You forgot something. To get everything, she had to lose everything first."

"But that's not the point."

"Then what *is* the point?"

"I don't know. When she wasn't here, everything was fine. Then she appears out of nowhere, and everyone wants to be with her. It seems everywhere I look, there she is."

One of the salespeople appeared at the office door, trying to get Nora's attention. Nora looked at Zoe. "Why don't you go through the book? There are a couple more over there too." She pointed at a long, heavy wooden workbench that had been converted into a filing cabinet.

"Thanks, Mom." She went to look at the different titles.

Nora went to help the customer at the front of the gallery. Zoe picked up another book about the history of theater in Ville des

Saintes. She found Rose's name in the index in the back. She opened it to a section on a small community ballet company. Some of the dancers and directors had gone on to starring roles on Broadway and done choreography in Hollywood. She flipped through the pages and found some of the costumes designed for a couple of their ballets. One was *A Midsummer's Night Dream*. The caption mentioned Rose by name.

Zoe looked at a dancer in a fairy costume. It looked familiar. She turned the page and saw a man in a military-style costume. She'd seen that one too. It took a few minutes. She remembered Autumn's sketchbook. These two costumes were the same as the ones Autumn had drawn and claimed as her own designs!

No. She hadn't said they were hers. The gymnast's costumes she said were based on what the kid in the park had wanted, but she hadn't said anything about these two. These were the same costumes, but the performers weren't in the same poses as they had been in her drawings. Maybe they weren't the same. Maybe they were just very similar. She'd show the book to Taylor and see what she thought.

"Did you find what you needed?" Nora said, going back to her desk.

"Yeah, these are great." Zoe quickly closed the book. "Can I take these home with me?"

Nora nodded, as she pulled a couple of binders out of the workbench. "You might want to look through these too. They're some of the postcards and ads that were sent out when the gallery first opened and some for different art shows we hosted or sponsored." Nora looked at the knapsack. "I guess I can bring them home with me tonight."

"Thanks, Mom. Do you want me to do anything to start dinner?"

"You can check on the stew in the slow cooker and stir it a couple of times."

Zoe put her knapsack on her shoulders. "Mom, do you remember what Oya was the Goddess of?"

Nora paused for a moment. "Thunderstorms, hurricanes, and... cemeteries."

Zoe kissed her mother's cheek. "I'll see you at home."

Zoe walked back through the gallery and waved at the receptionist. She made way for some deliverymen bringing in some rebar and glass shelving units.

Oya, Voodoo Goddess of Cemeteries. Well, it explained the creepy project.

utumn peeked over the upstairs railing. "Was that the doorbell?"

"No," said Kali. "I will send Zoe right up the stairs when she gets here. I promise."

Autumn went through a door disguised with chair-rail molding and paint to look like it was part of the wall. She flipped the light switch and went up the short flight of stairs to the attic. She'd been as jumpy as a frog with the hiccups since Zoe had called last night, confirming she would be coming to look through the photographs and papers. This had been Zoe's grandparents' home. Would Zoe still feel comfortable being here? Autumn tried not to feel like an interloper, but it wasn't easy.

Autumn had made some headway through the mess of papers and boxes, but she felt she hadn't even made a dent. She'd found the boxes of holiday decorations and moved them into one corner. Book-keeping files from the gallery were placed on a set of industrial metal shelves not far from the small round window. She'd have to ask Nora about those, but she'd make sure Nora knew she could store them in the attic for as long as she liked. There was some old furniture and old toys.

But the winners, in Autumn's opinion, were the huge steamer trunks. Some were the kind you could still get in a high-end department store. Others were antiques; almost like dressers, with places for hanging jackets and drawers for sweaters and undergarments. The trunks were great on their own, but they were full of clothes from every possible era. Either they were collected for costumes, or her family had kept every favorite piece of clothing since the 1800s. She couldn't wait to show them to Zoe and Taylor.

In one small leather suitcase, she found an antique camera. The label in the case said it was from 1890. It was in great condition; like a work of steampunk art all on its own.

When she began to uncover the collection of cameras she had inherited, she was in awe. It was all she could do to keep from creating an installation in the living room. They were all on one of the shelves now, safe and secure.

Maybe Zoe would want them since she loved photography so much. Maybe they could create some still-life compositions together like they used to. Wait. Autumn had never created any art with Zoe. They only met earlier that month. Maybe it was the ghost putting ideas in her head. That had to be the reason she thought of it as a memory.

Beneath an old desk, Autumn found boxes of photo binders and negatives, all organized by year, and by decade. There were more boxes and photo albums inside the desk drawers. Thank heavens Edward was careful with those.

Rose had painstakingly labeled each photo with the year, the location where it was taken, and who was in the picture. Each shelf of photos was now categorized and easily accessible. Autumn took a step back to survey the wall of boxes. The question now became, how far back to go? The box of photos from Eddie's parents should go to Nora and Zoe. She'd ask Uncle Theo to help Zoe take them back with her if she wanted to take them home. She pulled the box off the shelf and set it on the floor near the door. She sat down beside it, opened the box, and pulled out one of their albums.

Eddie's grandparents' photos were in an album tucked against the side of the box. His parents' wedding photo was on the first page of an album with a faded leather cover. Zoe had her paternal grandmother's eyes. Autumn turned the page to find some of Eddie's baby pictures, including the obligatory bathtub shot.

There weren't any baby pictures of Rose. She searched everywhere but only managed to find one of herself. It had been carefully wrapped in a wooden box in an old dresser beside the shelves. She opened the box and ran her fingers over the tarnished silver frame. It must have been taken at a carnival or something. She remembered seeing these types of photos taken at amusement parks, where the subjects got to choose costumes from the Old West or the 1920s. The photos were printed in black and white and sometimes had a blue or golden tint to them. This photo must have set her father back a couple of bob. It was well-crafted, it looked like it was ancient, and the background and costumes made it seem like it had been taken in an English home during the Victorian era. Her father was in an old-style military uniform, and Autumn sat on her mother's lap, a drowsy two-year-old, content and half-asleep. Her mother wore a long gown, and she was smiling. She was so ill, and she was still able to smile. Autumn blinked back tears. She wrapped the photo back up and put it away. Zoe didn't need to see that one.

Autumn opened a box labeled "1960 to 1975". There were loose papers and ticket stubs inside the box. Autumn found a program from an amateur production of *The Twelfth Night* dated July 29th–August 11th, 1966.

"Oh wow!" The mimeographed paper had started to yellow at the corners not protected by the binders above it. She carefully opened the booklet. There was Eddie's name and photo in the list of actors. He had played Malvolio, the servant of Lady Olivia.

Autumn found Rose's name and image in a group photo of the stage and design crew. Of course! This was when Rose and Eddie met. This was proof the vision she'd had in the park was real. It's the story the ghost had shown her. Autumn couldn't wait to show Zoe the program and see if she had heard the story from her grandparents. It might be an interesting angle for the installation: *Rose and Edward Sterling—the Art They Weren't So Famous For.*

Zoe stood in the entry hall of Rowan House, feeling too much like a guest. She hadn't been back since her grandparents died. The house was the same, but it wasn't. Grandpa Eddie wouldn't come down the stairs, singing an old song that had popped into his head. Grandma Rose wouldn't be at the dining room door, welcoming them to high tea.

High tea with Grandma Rose wasn't nearly as much fun as preparing for high tea with Grandma Rose. Zoe and Rose would go to the Salvation Army and the discount store to find ribbons, buttons, and glittery jewelry to decorate the hats prepared for the occasion. Zoe and Nora would sit with Rose in her sewing room, laughing and talking, and burning their fingers with hot glue, to create the fascinators and chapeaux they would wear for their monthly Sunday Tea.

When the day came, Zoe and Nora would arrive early in the afternoon, dressed as if they were going to the Ritz. Grandpa would wear a tuxedo, complete with top hat and tails, and the ladies would wear their creations. They would sit in the dining room, eating cucumber sandwiches and little cakes, and drinking tea from china cups. Grandpa Eddie made sure his little finger was always extended, even when he used his napkin. He would say things like "what ho" or "cheerio" and call everyone "old bean". Grandma Rose would smile or sometimes roll her eyes.

That's because Rose knew all about high tea. How could she have forgotten? Her British accent was hardly there anymore, but she would still call an elevator a "lift" or the trunk of the car the "boot". Something Zoe remembered, but never thought of in context. It was just Rose being Rose, not her grandmother being British.

Kali came out of the library and took both of Zoe's hands in hers. She found Autumn's godmother to be a very warm and caring woman. "Zoe, how good of you to come. Rose told me so much about you. It's nice to see you under more pleasant circumstances." She wore a beautiful sari; it was purple with embroidered silk flowers on the hem of her skirt and her shawl.

"Madam Kali. It's a pleasure to see you again".

Kali smiled. "Come, let us find Autumn Rose." She invited Zoe to take her arm. "Why so downhearted, little one?"

Zoe smiled sadly. "I remember coming here with Mom for high tea."

"Your grandmother loved those special Sundays and looked forward to them all month," Kali said.

"She talked to you about them?"

"All the time. They were very special, not only because of your visit, but she always loved high tea." Kali looked at Zoe. "Your grandmother was born in India but returned to her parent's home in England after her mother died. High tea was one of the traditions her father carried from country to country to country."

Rose was born in India? Didn't Autumn say that's where she was born?"

Autumn stood on the stairs, holding a file box. "Hello Zoe. Where's Taylor?"

"She couldn't get away, but I'm meeting her at the McCord University library tomorrow afternoon. Want to come with?"

"I can't. Kali wants me to run some errands for her. I guess you'll be the one stuck in the middle. But today won't be a lost day at all. You have to come and see everything I've found up here. It's like Aladdin's cave."

"Cool!"

"I've moved some of the boxes of photos and papers into the library so we can use the scanner and the computer."

"Great idea." Searching closets and hauling boxes down from the attic was something Grandma Rose would have done. There would also be a new package of paper beside the printer and an unopened ink cartridge in case of emergency. The scanner would be beside the computer, ready to go.

Zoe opened the library door. The scanner had been taken from the shelf and plugged into a laptop. There was a box of paper on the floor. The plastic strapping still held the lid closed. A bag from *Inks, Books, and Cables*, Rose's favorite office supply store, sat on top of the desk. Zoe looked at Autumn and tried to smile. "Everything is perfect."

Autumn put her box on a bridge table set up in the middle of the room. Coincidence? Maybe overpreparing was a genetic thing. Zoe watched as Autumn twisted her hair into a bun and secured it with an unsharpened pencil—something Grandma Rose always did; something Zoe also learned to do. Rose wasn't here anymore, but she was all over Rowan House. Zoe didn't think being here would be this hard.

"You have to see what I found." Autumn opened the box and pulled out a fuchsia fascinator decorated with mauve netting and rhinestone broaches. "Isn't this beautiful? Oh, and look at this." She pulled out a black top hat and popped it open.

Zoe just couldn't do it anymore. She sat down on the floor and started to cry.

Autumn put her arms around her. "What's happened? What's the matter?"

Zoe spoke through her sobs. She told Autumn about Sunday Tea with her grandparents. About making the hats, and how the one Autumn had taken from the box had been the last one she had made with Rose. "I stopped wanting to come over. I felt it was silly baby stuff. And now, we'll never have another chance to be together."

"Oh honey. I'm so, so sorry."

"It's not fair. She was an artist, with works in the National Gallery. I should have learned all these things about her *from* her. Not from a bunch of books. And you got shafted too. We could have known about each other when she was still alive. We could have grown up together. You and your father could have come to the tea parties and dressed up and made cool hats."

Autumn pulled away. "It never would have happened. My father traveled a lot for his work, and my stepmother would never do anything frivolous." Autumn looked at the boxes on the table. There were tears in her eyes now too.

Zoe took Autumn's hand. "But maybe if your father had known

about Rose and Eddie after your mother died, he wouldn't have felt so alone. He would have known there was family to help."

Autumn nodded. "Maybe he wouldn't have felt like he had to marry such a capable woman. Maybe he would have found someone else out of love and joy instead of duty."

"The way our grandmother did," Zoe said.

They sat together on the floor, lost in thought, sharing a box of tissues.

Thanatos knocked on the door and asked them if they wanted some refreshments. "I can make some tea, and the sandwiches Rose used to make."

Zoe felt her throat close with tears.

"Uncle Theo, could you please order a pizza for us?" She looked at Zoe. "Pizza? All dressed? With everything but the kitchen sink?"

She wiped her eyes. "No anchovies."

"Everything but anchovies and the kitchen sink," Autumn said. "We're starting a new tradition for cousin get-togethers."

"And I guess there will be ice cream floats for dessert?" Uncle Theo asked.

"Of course," said Zoe. "Thank you." Uncle Theo went in search of pizza. Zoe took a deep breath. "Okay, now let's get to work."

Autumn stood up and went to the boxes she had brought down from the attic. "The photo albums are in this box. They're labeled by year. I found a box of photos of Eddie and his family. I found some of the gallery's files as well. You can take the photos and papers home with you if you'd like. Or you and your mom can store them here. It's not like there's not enough room."

"Thanks. I'll call her later and ask. But we should go through the box to see if there's anything to inspire the installation."

Autumn pointed out another set of boxes. "To that end, I've found scrapbooks and marketing plans in these two boxes, and those, over there, have lots of envelopes. I think they might be letters."

Zoe took her binder from her knapsack. "Did you find anything on Rose's early life?"

"Nothing yet. I'll go back up to the attic and keep looking if you're okay here."

"I'm fine," Zoe said. "After the pizza, I think we should work upstairs together."

"Sounds good to me." Autumn left to go to the attic.

Zoe thought she'd start with the photo albums. She sat down on the floor, but the lid on the box seemed to be stuck. So she moved on to the next box.

*Oh well, start with the letters.* But there weren't any letters in the box. There were manila envelopes and file folders. The first envelope was from a lawyer and had Autumn Rose's name on it, but it was addressed to someplace in British Columbia. Someone had written "Will" on the envelope. After checking to see if there was anyone around, Zoe opened the envelope.

It was the *Last Will and Testament for Autumn Rose Cassidy*, and it was dated 1937. But that was before her grandmother was even born. She flipped through the document. It mentioned Rowan House and some other properties. She stopped and read the next page. The Autumn Rose who had written this will also had a son who was raised by relatives in another country. And this 1937 woman was leaving her entire estate to her granddaughter and namesake, Autumn Rose—Zoe's grandmother. But if Rose had been born in 1948, how did this woman know about her?

She put the will back in the envelope and found a folder with baptismal and birth certificates in it. Four of them. Each one announced Autumn Rose Cassidy, born in India, was a citizen of Great Britain and the Commonwealth. Each one had the same name. Each one had the same place of birth. Each named the same parents, including her mother's maiden name. But they were all from different decades.

She pulled out the folder of wills again to see if they matched. It was the same story each time: a grandmother named Autumn Rose had an estranged son who was deceased. Then, the grandmother leaves her estate to her granddaughter and namesake, Autumn Rose. At least the lawyer's name was different on each will. Unless...

She used her phone to look up the name of the lawyer who created the last will. The document had been signed on August 1st, 1965. The man died in a car accident on July 15th, 1965. Zoe tried to look up the name on an earlier document, but the lawyer wasn't listed online.

She glanced at the door, as she quickly shoved the folder filled with papers and the envelope of wills into her school bag. It had to be a clerical error. She'd show it to Taylor, who would tell her she had been reading too many Stephen King novels, and everything would be right with the world again.

Her hands shook as she closed the box and opened the one filled with photos. The dates on the albums meant these were from her grandparents' lifetime. A couple of older albums had ended up in the wrong box. They were dated from around the First World War. Thinking she would find photos of Eddie's or Rose's parents, she opened one of the albums. A woman was standing beside an antique car—antique in Zoe's lifetime, anyway. The woman's face was a bit blurry, but not enough for Zoe to fail to recognize her cousin, or at least what she'd look like in a few years. There was another album dated 1910, with a photo of some women standing by a sign for St. Maurice Veterans Hospital, the year it had opened. Her grandmother was in that photo.

She found another photo of some nurses, some nuns, and some men in white coats near the main door of St. Katherine's. Zoe used her phone to magnify and photograph the women in the picture. The second from the left was Autumn … but it couldn't be. But it was. Zoe took another photo as a copy of the whole picture. The album from 1910 was the oldest in the box.

She heard voices in the hallway, closed the box, and stood beside the albums from her grandfather's lifetime.

The door opened. "I found some of the yearbooks and posters from Eddie and Rose's school days." Autumn set another box on the floor. "This one has stuff that will blow your mind!"

"I honestly believe my mind will never be any more blown than it will be today."

Autumn giggled and showed Zoe the scrapbook of playbills. Zoe smiled and fired up the computer. "We got some scanning to do."

146

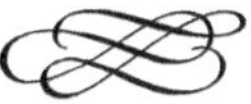

Zoe ran up to Taylor. "Sorry I'm late."

"No problem." Taylor watched as a handsome male university student walked up the library's stairs. "I had street scenes to keep me occupied."

"I bet. Inspirational? Artistically, I mean."

"Definitely. Artistic inspiration is everywhere."

Zoe smiled. "My dad called as I was leaving." Taylor and Zoe made their way up the stairs and past the stone lions gracing the entrance to the McCord University library.

"Bothering your mom for money from your grandfather's estate again?"

"Not this time. He's going to be in New York on business in March, and he wants me to meet him there."

"That's cool."

"It's not. It's cold. It means I'll be there for my mother's birthday. Her first without her parents to help celebrate." The warm building was a relief from the damp October day. "He's put me in a no-win situation. I go to New York, and I feel like crap for abandoning my mother. I refuse to go, and it's my fault I don't see him after he clearly made the effort to reach out to me."

"But he didn't do anything special. He was going to New York anyway. Right?" Taylor pointed to an empty table in a closed meeting room. They'd be able to talk quietly in there. "He might be in the same time zone, but it's still another country. New York is an hour or so by plane. Is he sending you a ticket to fly there?"

"He didn't say."

"He's the adult with all the air miles. Besides, won't you need a letter of permission and a passport to cross the border by yourself?"

Zoe nodded. "You're right. I'll text him tonight and suggest he come here. Thanks, Tay."

Zoe closed the door as Taylor put her knapsack on the table.

"So now that we're here Zoe," Taylor asked, "what's the big secret you couldn't talk about over the phone?"

Zoe took the envelope and folder she'd taken from Rowan House out of her bag and pulled out the wills and other papers. They looked so surreal in the harsh neon lighting. "All of these certificates have the name Autumn Rose Cassidy on them. All the Autumn Roses were born in India to Elizabeth Marie Grail and James Cassidy of Kent, England. This is a copy of my grandmother's will. The lawyer created it about a week after he died."

"You mean before he died."

"No. I mean after."

"Maybe the month got confused with the day like the sixth of July being mistaken for the seventh of June."

"The date on the documents, even the baptismal certificates, is always at the end of October."

"You're right. It is very weird." Taylor picked up one of the wills. "So, do you want to see if the same is true for the rest of the notaries and lawyers?"

"Yes. And there's more weirdness. Each of these wills was created for someone named Autumn Rose Cassidy. Each of the wills says she was married and divorced or widowed, and there's a son named James from the marriage who lives with relatives out of the country."

"What country is her son in?"

"Doesn't matter. He's always in a country she's not in." Zoe opened one of the documents and pointed to something on the page. "The will leaves everything in Autumn Rose's estate to the mysterious James and his heirs."

Zoe flipped to the end of the document. "On the last page of the will, there's a copy of the mystery son's death certificate and a memorandum and codicil that names his daughter, Autumn Rose Cassidy, his sole heir and beneficiary."

"Your mom's secret brother is dead?"

"To tell the truth, I don't think he was ever alive. Not as her brother anyway." Zoe took out her phone and showed Taylor some of the photos she'd copied at Rowan House. "See? They all look like Grandma Rose or Autumn."

Taylor pointed to the photo of the hospital staff in front of their school. "I've seen that photo before. It's in the administration building, across from my dad's office. It's a grouping of the school's history. The photo was taken when the convent was converted to a hospital during the Spanish Flu pandemic."

"You've seen it, but have you really looked at it?" She zoomed in on the face of one of the nurses. "See?"

"That means there's a strong genetic connection."

"This is more than a family resemblance. It has to be. There are no variations. They all have the same hair, and skin, and face. It can't just be genetics."

"What are you saying?"

"I don't know what I'm saying. I think I'm losing it." She dropped into the chair and lay her head on the table, the way they'd been taught in kindergarten.

Taylor put her hand on Zoe's shoulder. "If you're worried about your sanity, don't. I hate to break it to you, but that boat sailed a long time ago." Zoe picked up her head and gave Taylor *the look*. Taylor shrugged. "Zoe, we're artists. Normal isn't our way of being."

"But what about all this?"

"We definitely have a mystery here. Do you think she's a clone?"

"Can't be. These papers go back to the nineteenth century. She would have to be an alien to have that kind of technology in the 1800s."

"Alien was my next guess."

"Seriously? That would make me one-quarter Martian."

"Well..." Laughing, Taylor jumped back before Zoe could hit her. Taylor sat down in the chair beside Zoe and took her hands. "What was the line from Sherlock Holmes? That once you've sorted through all the crap, the result—despite being batshit crazy—is probably the right answer."

"Something like that, but he didn't phrase it quite so elegantly."

"The point is, we need more information. We have to think logically."

Zoe sighed. "Logic went out the window when I got to the fourth Autumn Rose."

*Taylor* looked over Zoe's shoulder. "That's the last of them," Zoe said. "All of these wills were created by dead men." Beginning with the first, dated 1878, to the one belonging to her grandmother, created in 1967. "The first Autumn Rose's father was awarded land by the Crown in 1863. We didn't become our own country until 1867."

"This is so weird." Taylor spread the papers out to see the dates. "Autumn Rose has been in Canada since before Canada was Canada." Taylor sat down beside Zoe. "But they can't all be the same person."

"My grandmother's naturalization certificate is dated 1964." She pointed at another certificate, dated January 2017. "This has to be my cousin's."

"It means she's been somewhere in Canada for almost a year."

"Worse than that. They don't hand these things out at the airport. To even be able to apply, she'd have to have been in Canada for something like five years or more."

"So where has she been all this time?"

"She's been here since she was at least twelve, and my grandmother never once introduced her to the family, never said where she was staying. Mom only found out about her when Eddie made the change to his will, naming my mother as Autumn's guardian should anything happen to him."

"But you knew your grandmother. I'm sure she had a good reason."

Zoe thought back to when she was twelve, seeing her father off on a business trip only to discover he was never coming back from Hong Kong. "You're right. My grandmother could not have been so cruel. Rose would never have let Autumn fend for herself in a strange country while her family was practically next door." She looked out the window at the students walking through the library, but she didn't see them. "At least I hope she wouldn't do that. Truthfully, I don't think I knew Rose at all."

Zoe lay on her bed, staring at the ceiling. A Canadian history textbook lay open across her stomach. Nothing about her grandmother's life made any sense. They had found a passenger list with Rose's name on it, but the ship had landed in Ville des Saints over a century ago. The document said Autumn Rose Cassidy was a 45-year-old nurse returning from England after teaching there for over a decade before the First World War.

She rolled over. How could they all be named Autumn Rose? Names were passed down in families, true. But then there was the freaky bit. They were all born in India, they all had parents named Elizabeth and James, and they all looked alike.

There were three possibilities, and each sounded crazier than the last. Zoe had overruled Taylor's theory about aliens, only because the line had to be drawn someplace.

Option one: Rose was a time traveler. Nope. If she was, she wouldn't have looked as old as her grandmother. And she would have saved Grandpa Eddie from going over the cliff. She loved him. If she could travel through time, she would have gone back, and neither of them would have gotten into the car. Rose would have finished her cancer treatment, and gone into remission again, and they would both be alive and well and planning the big gallery show.

Option two: She was a clone, and there was an Autumn Rose farm someplace in India. That meant they were releasing a new Autumn Rose every century or so. That didn't make any sense either. What would be their motivation? Where would they have gotten the technology to clone someone in the 1800s? And who the hell was doing the cloning?

She was left with one last option. No, it was too ridiculous. Maybe Taylor was right. Maybe Rose was from another planet. It was easier than thinking her grandmother was an immortal with epic disguise skills.

If Rose was immortal, there had to be some kind of proof. There had to be a stash of makeup and wigs someplace at Rowan House.

Zoe sat up. Was immortality genetic? Would she live forever too? But if it was hereditary, why did her mother have a heart problem? The last photo she'd taken of her grandparents was tucked into the mirror on her dresser.

Something was missing. Makeup could be good, but she'd seen her grandmother up close, without a hint of anything on her face. Rose had taken her swimming, for crying out loud. No matter how fit her grandmother was, she didn't have the body of a sixteen-year-old, and Autumn wasn't shaped like an old woman.

"Zoe! I'm home!" Nora called as her footsteps hit the creaky spot on the wood floor. Nora waved as she passed Zoe's bedroom door. "How's the project going?"

"Pretty good. Are we still going to brunch with Autumn and the Mains next Sunday?"

"Zoe?" Nora stood in her doorway. "What do you think about taking an afternoon off from work, and we all go see the Botanical Garden after brunch?"

"Yeah, sounds great." Zoe closed her book and followed her mother to the kitchen to help prepare dinner. "I'll bring my camera."

"I'm sure Rose would be happy to see her two granddaughters getting along."

A few months ago, Zoe would have agreed, but when it came to Grandma Rose, she wasn't sure of anything anymore.

Zoe tossed her soda can into the recycle bin and headed for the student lounge to do some reading. Part of her was thinking about different class assignments she had coming up. But every thought seemed to circle back to her grandmother's secret life. She was so lost in thought she didn't notice Autumn until she put her hand on Zoe's shoulder.

"I'm sorry," said Autumn. "I didn't mean to startle you."

"It's okay. I like getting my heart jump-started after lunch. Easier than doing cardio in the gym." They walked over to one of the window seats that looked out onto the building which housed the art gallery and the theater. Zoe thought they would talk about the big installation, but they ended up sitting in silence, their books still in their respective bags.

Autumn leaned over so their shoulders touched. "Want to talk about it?"

"I don't know if I can." Especially if it meant confessing to taking all those legal documents out of Autumn's house. She sighed. "I've been finding out things about my—sorry—our—grandmother I never knew and she never talked about. I thought I knew her, but when I think about it, I hardly knew her at all. I mean, I can tell you stories about Eddie and his parents and his growing up in the '60s. He had a story for every occasion. But I don't even know Rose's maiden name, or anything about her parents, or what inspired her art, or anything. It's so damned frustrating."

"I understand, and unfortunately, I can't help you. I remember even less about her than you do."

"Let's start with something you can help with. Can you tell me about your grandfather? You know, your father's father. He was Rose's first husband. What was he like?"

Autumn thought for a moment. "I don't remember much about my grandfather, Nigel Cassidy. He was British but lived in Jamaica. We stopped there to visit on our way to Canada. I was a kid when I met him, and we didn't stay there long. My father and his father didn't seem to agree on anything. Grandfather Cassidy met my stepmother when my father started dating her and thought she was a gold-digger. He was right, of course. But my father didn't want to see it. I think he ended up marrying her out of spite." She shrugged her shoulders. "What I remember about him is he was tall. He towered over everyone, including my father. He had a booming laugh. If he heard something funny, he would explode with this baritone, 'Ho, ho, ho.' My dad's laugh was really quiet. His mouth would be open, and you'd see his belly shaking, but there was hardly any sound at all."

"What do you think Rose saw in him?"

"He was ambitious. When Nigel Cassidy decided on something, he went and got it. My father said he moved to Jamaica because he was tired of the English rain. He wasn't a young man when my father was born, so he was probably a lot older than Rose when they met."

"What did he do?"

"Grandfather Cassidy was a lawyer if I remember correctly. Contract law, or estate law, or something like that."

Zoe could see the story forming. "Here comes your grandfather. He's successful. He's a lawyer, or at least a law student when they meet."

"And there was family money there too."

"Okay. He has a couple of bucks. Rose is a young girl. Impressionable. Nigel's confident and well-off. She sees him as someone who wants to take care of her and give her a good life, so they marry."

Autumn nods. "Makes sense. They live together for a while. His caring becomes smothering. She wants to be an artist, but he wants her to be a fashion accessory on his climb up the social register. She decides the only way to stay sane is to leave."

Zoe gasps. "He won't let her take their son away with her. He needs the heir apparent to show his friends his superior genes. So he, what? Blackmails Rose? Leave our son or no divorce? If you want any money from me, you'll leave our kid?"

"Or maybe he told her to leave without anything more than what she could carry in a single suitcase. Or maybe she escaped in the middle of the night. She leaves without any money. She has no home to go back to. She had no choice but to leave her son behind, or take him with, and risk having him placed in care."

They both sighed. "How terrible," Zoe said. "It's the saddest story I've ever heard."

"Zoe, I'm glad she found Eddie. She deserved to be happy after such a loveless marriage."

"And they were so happy together." She blinked away the tears. "My grandfather could be a joker, or super-serious, but he always lit up like a firecracker when Rose was with him."

The two sat in silence. The sunlight cast their shadows on the floor and set the dust motes shining like fireflies.

Jacob and Joshua saw the cousins sitting there. Josh nodded toward them and said, "So, are you two meditating, or communing with ghosts?"

Jake smiled, and said a quick hello to Zoe, but greeted Autumn so warmly, it was as if he hadn't seen her in years.

"There is no such thing as ghosts," Zoe said.

"What ghosts are you talking about?" Autumn asked at the same time.

"Bad news is that the school is haunted," Jake said. "But the good news is that they seldom come down this hallway. They stay around the cafeteria."

"Those noises in the caf aren't ghosts, Jake," Zoe said. "Unless someone is being haunted by the indigestion of lunches past." Zoe turned to Autumn. "Would heartburn be considered a haunting, or would it count more as a possession?"

"I guess you'd save on the cost of an exorcism by using antacids." Autumn waved her hands in front of the twins and, lowering her voice, she said, *"Avaunt, thou dreadful minister of hell. Thou hadst but power over his mortal body; his soul thou canst not have. Therefore begone."*

Jake burped and started blushing. The girls and Joshua laughed.

"Not the usual reaction to Shakespeare's *Richard III*." Autumn shrugged one shoulder. "But, whatever."

Jake mumbled goodbye, and Joshua rolled his eyes as his brother led him away.

"Smooth move there Jake."

"Shut up."

They still argued as they turned the corner.

"Okay," Autumn said once they were out of view. "What's all this about ghosts in the school?"

"It's dumb. It's an old building, with old pipes and old windows. People hear weird noises, so it has to be ghosts. You don't believe in ghosts, do you?"

Autumn was silent for a moment. "I kind of do. I've experienced some strange things in my travels and also at Rowan House. It's hard to explain."

"My grandparents' house is haunted?" She laughed. "I think I would have noticed before now."

"I better be getting on to class." Autumn stood up and lifted her bag off the floor. "I'll see you later."

"Wait!" Zoe grabbed her bag and followed Autumn down the hall. "Is the house haunted?"

Autumn stopped. "Yes. The house is haunted."

"By who?" Zoe turned Autumn so that she looked at her. "Who is it?"

Autumn looked at the ground. "I'm not sure. But it might be your grandfather."

"You're nuts!" Zoe could feel her temper rising. "My grandfather is gone." She stomped away. Turned and came back. "How dare you! Who do you think you are? You didn't know them. You're just a stranger pretending to be my family. You have a bloody nerve!" Zoe ran down the hall, her eyes filling with tears of anger and grief. She heard Autumn calling after her. Zoe ducked into the washroom and shut herself into an empty stall.

Eddie and Rose were gone. They had died together. He would never have come back to Earth without her. He would never have left her to come back to haunt an old house.

*utumn closed the car door. Uncle Theo had tried to talk to her about her day, but she hadn't been able to clear the lump in her throat long enough to get anything out.

The day had gone from bad to worse. First, Zoe was upset about the ghost of her grandfather being in Rowan House. Jake was so embarrassed about burping during her recitation from *Richard III*, that he wouldn't even look at her in French class. She tried to talk to Taylor about their next meeting for the installation, but she wouldn't stop running long enough to even set a time to talk about talking, let alone actually meeting.

"What's happened, *Koukla*? You're not yourself at all."

She shrugged. Maybe Kali had been right all along. Autumn wasn't like regular people. Maybe she should pack everything up and move back to Kent, or her grandfather's house in Jamaica. She could learn what she needed to from books, or from one of the Fates she had met in the park. There were online courses, too. She could graduate from high school that way. She didn't need a career. She had her work with Kali.

That's what she'd do. Once they were home, she'd talk to Kali about leaving and living someplace else, someplace where she wouldn't have to worry about her memory. She could put Rowan House up for sale. Or maybe let Nora have it. It was more a part of her legacy than it would ever be Autumn's. She leaned her head back against the car seat. A tear slid down her cheek.

"*Koukla mou*. Why are you so sad?"

Autumn wiped her eyes with the heel of her palm. "I think I may have hurt Zoe. Badly. I don't think she'll ever speak to me again."

"Maybe you are overreacting a little bit. She's a nice girl. What could you have said that would be so terrible, she couldn't forgive you?"

"I told her our house was haunted... by her grandfather."

"Ah." Thanatos nodded and thought for a bit. "It was probably not a good idea."

"Because you don't believe he's here either?"

"Oh no. He's here. We had coffee together this morning." Autumn's mouth dropped open. He continued. "You shouldn't have told her because she misses him so much. For you to be able to speak to him, while she can't, is breaking her heart."

"I can invite her over, and she can talk to him for hours if she wants. Is there a way that she can see him?"

He signaled to turn into their driveway. "You know how you see ghosts using your special jewelry and the separating oil? Well, if you have the oil on your hand, and hold her hand with the same hand that has the oil, she can see spirits too."

"Could we make a chain? I hold her hand, and she can hold Nora's. Or can I put the oil on each hand? Would they both be able to talk to Eddie Sterling?"

"If Zoe has the oil on her hand and holds her mother's hand, she will be able to see the ghosts too. But one of them has to hold your hand, or they won't see much." He opened the car door. "And one thing that's very important. You must never, ever, tell Kali I told you. Okay? She wouldn't understand."

Autumn agreed and went up the stairs. Ideas began to take shape. This could be a way to show Zoe that she was serious about talking to ghosts, and it would also help whoever was haunting the school. She called hello to Kali and went up to her room. She had some phone calls to make.

## THURSDAY, OCTOBER 18TH, 2017

*A*utumn paced in front of the Special Projects class. She checked her watch. As far as Zoe and Taylor knew, she'd asked them to meet her early because she'd found something very important that would change their project. It was her first time wearing any of her enchanted jewelry to school. Autumn saw people walking through the hallway. Their *Ka* followed behind them, instructing them on their homework or reminding them to grab some food before class.

"Hi Autumn," said Taylor.

"We're here," said Zoe. "What's so Earth-shattering?"

"I found out where the school's ghosts hang out, and I want to help them move on to the afterlife. I thought you might want to come and help."

"Seriously?" Zoe rolled her eyes. "That's what was so urgent? You want us to take time away from our project and go play Ghostbusters?"

"That would be so cool," Taylor said. "Will it work with only the three of us, or do we need a bigger group?

"Count me out," said Zoe. "Some of us have work to do. Come on Taylor."

"If you don't want to come, that's your choice. I'll go help the ghosts on my own then, shall I?"

"Wait," Taylor said. "I want to help."

"Help with what?" Joshua said as he started to head into the room. Jake mumbled his hello.

"Nothing important," Zoe said.

"We're going to have a séance." Taylor could hardly control her excitement. "We're going to clear out the school's ghosts! Isn't that cool?"

"Very cool." Oya Bridges stood behind them. Autumn almost jumped out of her skin. The others looked as if they had been startled as well. "Just make sure you know what you're doing. The dead don't always believe they're dead."

The same holy glow that had been around Kali and Thanatos was around Ms. Bridges. Oya was an Agent of Death.

Autumn tried to smile. "Don't worry. We'll remember to be careful."

Oya nodded. "Don't be too long out here. We'll be starting soon." She went into the classroom.

"I swear, that woman has crazy ninja skills," said Taylor. "We have to get her some bangles, or a bell, or squeaky shoes, or something that lets us know she's standing behind us."

"It won't work," Zoe said. "She's the Voodoo Goddess of Cemeteries. You know how quiet those places are. She can't help herself."

"Seriously?" asked Jake.

"I think the correct term is Orisha," said Autumn thoughtfully. "But yes. Oya is the name of the Orisha of thunderstorms and cemeteries."

Jacob and Joshua looked at each other.

"So, when does this séance start?" Josh said.

"You two aren't invited," Zoe said.

Autumn crossed her arms. "And I thought you weren't interested."

"This is our project," Taylor said. "I think we should decide together if outsiders should be included."

"If you'll excuse us." Zoe took Autumn and Taylor away from the doorway. She turned her back to the twins. "Autumn, are you sure that we'll be able to talk to the ghosts?"

Autumn nodded. "I'm sure." She looked at each of the girls. "Should we include Jacob and Joshua?"

"I say no," Taylor said. "They only want to come with because we told them they're not allowed."

Zoe agreed. "They enjoy stirring things up. If we tell them where we're going to meet, they'll tell as many people as they can and try to sell tickets."

"Really?" Autumn asked.

"They wanted to work on the Sterlings as their special project," Zoe said. "They were selling raffle tickets to see who would work with them."

"What made them think they would get the assignment? Especially with you already in the class."

"Their uncle, Walter Kempt, had some weird connection to the gallery back in the day," Taylor said. "Zo, tell her what they said about your grandparents."

Zoe put her hand on Autumn's arm. "According to their uncle, Rowan House was a hotbed of drugs and orgies."

Autumn looked over her shoulder at the twins. "Their uncle was an overpriced, incompetent dog walker. He didn't even have the brains God gave a grapefruit." She turned back. "Please never mention that little nugget to Madam Kali. She loved Rose like a sister, and if she found out what they said…. Well, if their uncle isn't dead, he will be. And it will not be pretty." Autumn could picture his sour, acne-covered face as another bead on Auntie-ji's necklace, and she shuddered.

"I'll go tell them," Taylor said. "I enjoy bursting their balloons."

Zoe looked thoughtfully at Autumn. "Where and when."

"The H-wing. Second floor. The instruments storage room. Study period."

*Z*oe had always loved photo-retouching class, but now all she could do was watch the clock. She would be meeting Taylor and Autumn in the H-building, right after this class. The bell finally rang, and she was on her way.

She rarely went to this wing of the school. It housed the drama and music departments. Technically, the building should have been the F-building. But the school had decided to keep the 'H' to honor when this had been the hospital wing of the convent attached to the church. Even the building had been kept more or less intact than other parts of the school. The stairs in this part of the building were still made of oak, instead of stone, and the railings were iron and rope instead of wood. Zoe followed the hallway to the instrument storage room. Autumn was there, waiting.

"Taylor's gone to get the key from the department office," Autumn said, her hands stuffed into her jacket pockets.

"What excuse did she give them for wanting the key?"

"Something about needing to draw or photograph some instruments, so that she can use them as part of a movie poster."

"I'm here." Taylor's sneakers squeaked against the floor as she ran toward them. "I've got the key." She stopped to catch her breath and unlocked the door.

Autumn found the switch and turned on the light. The room was bigger than Zoe imagined. And a lot quieter. Students were in the classrooms all around them, but you wouldn't know it because of all the soundproofing. Guitars, violins, and ukuleles hung on the walls. Large basses and violas were suspended from the ceiling. There were a couple of pianos and a large harp under some beige drop cloths on the far side of the room. Shelves held percussion instruments, horns, mouthpieces, and small boxes of strings, resins, reeds, and drumsticks.

There were two banks of filing cabinets in the center of the room. Zoe opened a drawer and saw files of sheet music.

"Where do we start?" Taylor asked.

Autumn looked around the room as if waiting for someone else to show up. "How about we move these piano stools over there, where we'll have room to sit together."

"Now what," said Zoe. She still felt ridiculous, although she wanted to come back here with her camera. The light, the shapes, and the shadows would make some great black-and-white photos.

Autumn took a beautiful egg-shaped gemstone out of her pocket. Zoe thought it was solid and was surprised when Autumn opened a stopper. She poured a few drops of the liquid from the bottle into the palm of each of the girl's hands and showed them how to rub it in.

"This smells amazing," said Zoe.

"It's a very special blend used only for helping spirits leave the Earth," said Autumn.

"Is there any danger? To us, I mean?" asked Taylor. "You know, having this stuff on our hands?"

"Except we're not ghosts," said Zoe.

"All right." Autumn invited the girls to sit down on their piano stools. "First, we hold hands." Zoe took one of Autumn's hands and Taylor took the other. "Now we close our eyes." Zoe's ears were ringing. Her inner voice seemed to be louder. The room was silent. Autumn's voice broke her reverie. "Spirits, if you can hear me, please come show yourselves. We only want to help."

There were quiet footsteps somewhere behind her. Zoe felt something brush against her back. Taylor yipped when it passed her.

Familiar laughter broke her concentration. Zoe opened her eyes. The twins were doubled over, their eyes tearing.

"You should have seen your face when I touched you with the feather Zoe," Jacob said. "You were all like..." He made his mouth drop open and raised his eyebrows.

"But Taylor was better," said Joshua. He yipped, then bunched up his shoulders, looking like he had eaten something sour. The two started laughing again. Taylor opened her eyes and gave the twins a look that should have turned them into ghosts.

"Stay focused ladies," said Autumn. "We have work to do and not a lot of time to do it."

A wind came through the room. Zoe looked around, but she didn't see anything.

Taylor was sitting with her eyes scrunched closed. "Did you feel that?"

"Taylor," Zoe whispered, "it's safe. The walls aren't bleeding or anything."

Taylor opened one eye, smiled, and looked like she was waiting for the show to start. The hairs on Zoe's arms started to stand up. She could see shadows coming and going through the room. She sat down and took Autumn's hand. Part of her wanted to believe it was the room's odd lighting being blocked by the instruments, but the shadows kept moving.

Taylor jumped from her seat, taking Autumn's hand with her. "Did you see that?"

A woman in a nun's habit carried a tray through the room, passing through the filing cabinets. She ignored the living people as she examined the things on her tray. Zoe nodded. The girls followed the ghost's movements with their eyes.

Jacob and Joshua looked around.

"There's nothing here," Josh said.

"Yes, there is," Zoe said as she watched two children pass through the wall. "You just don't have the skills or the potion."

"What potion?" Jake asked.

Taylor sighed as she returned to her seat. "Autumn, could you please give those two morons some of the stuff, so they can see what we're talking about?"

Zoe didn't know where to look first. People moved through the room without noticing the girls sitting in their path or each other. Her breath caught in her chest and she shivered when one of the spirits passed through her.

"You have to be willing to hold hands with each other," Autumn said as she looked at the twins and the girls. "Well?"

"You're trying to freak us out," Jake said.

"No," Taylor said. "It's all real, and it's fantastic!"

"We know when we're being had," said Josh. "Let's go Jake."

"Jake, you're going to miss something phenomenal, because your brother is afraid of girl cooties. I thought you had your own brain." Zoe looked into his eyes. "If you leave, Taylor's right. You are both morons."

He stepped closer to the circle. "Can I have some of the potion, please?"

Joshua made a face and left Jake in the room with the girls. Autumn stood up, got another stool, and set it between Zoe and Taylor. When Autumn let go of Zoe's hand to give Jake some potion, the vision of the ghosts faded a little. She could still see them, but not as clearly as when Autumn was holding her hand. When the circle was whole again, Zoe saw someone watching them from the doorway. She thought Joshua had come back, but when he stepped forward, she noticed he was in uniform.

"Well, well, well," said the soldier. "If it isn't Miss Archie. It's been a long time."

"Who's he talking to?" Zoe asked.

"I'm talking to the bearcat beside you, miss."

"What's a bearcat?" Jake asked.

"It's the Roaring '20s way of calling a woman a badass," said Taylor. She looked at Jake. "What? I read you know."

"Don't you remember me, Autumn Rose?" asked the soldier.

Autumn's breath caught in her chest.

Zoe looked at the soldier. "You must be thinking of our great-grandmother." She turned to her cousin. "The name Autumn Rose has been in the family since the 1800s."

Autumn seemed to be thinking about something. "We can talk about this later. Let's help the soldier."

"Not yet. I want to find out more about our ancestor." She turned to the soldier. "Excuse me, sir. How did you know Autumn Rose?"

"And why did you call her Archie?" asked Jake. "And a bearcat."

"You look exactly like her, though." He sighed. "The Autumn Rose Cassidy I knew worked in the hospital as a nurse's aide as part of her training. She came into the ward one day with her apron on inside out. The laundry mark read 'A.R.C.-H'. It was the same day she and the other sisters had to deal with a shellshock case who was being a bit feisty. She lowered her voice, so it sounded a bit more masculine and started ordering him around like she was his drill sergeant. The boy settled down, and the rest of us started calling her Archie."

"Because she had to pretend to be a man?" Taylor asked.

"That's what they told the head sister, but it wasn't true. Was it, Olivier?" Autumn said. "An Archie was what they called a British anti-aircraft gun."

Olivier laughed. "Yes, ma'am. Most of the women on the ward were nuns. But of the civilian and army nurses, Miss Autumn Rose was the youngest and the prettiest of the bunch. So she was always fending off unwanted attention. The truth was that she shot down more fliers and soldiers than the Kaiser ever could. And did it with more panache, skill, and accuracy, to boot. We told anyone who asked, the story about the shellshock and the apron. But us boys in the ward knew better."

"Why weren't you in the veteran's hospital?" said Zoe. She remembered the photo in her grandmother's scrapbook of an older woman standing in front of the sign at the opening of the Saint-Maurice Hospital.

"Because we had influenza and needed to be kept away from the others." The soldier wandered the room. "Some of us got better, but a lot of us died. Mustard gas and Spanish Flu don't make for a healthy man." He looked at the piano. "I used to play. I don't know why I never saw this here before."

Autumn stood up and went to him. Zoe could still make out the soldier, but he was more like an overexposed photo: the borders around his body faded into the surrounding room, and his face was so bright his features were almost invisible.

"I'm afraid it's time for you to go on to the afterlife," Autumn said. "The hospital is gone. This is part of a school now. I can help you if you'd like."

The soldier came close to Autumn. Zoe heard him talking, but couldn't understand what he was saying. Autumn looked shocked by what he said. He said something that made Autumn look sad, but she nodded in response. She poured some more of the oil from the bottle into her hand. The soldier reached into her palm. He became more solid. Autumn sat down and restored the circle. Zoe watched a golden light open in the wall. More ghosts came out of the opening. Taylor gasped. The spirits welcomed the soldier. He was hugged by some and shook hands with others.

The soldier turned. "Thank you, my beloved Miss Cassidy. I didn't realize how tired I was until I touched that oil in your hand. It's time that I went home." He followed the others back through the golden opening. When the last spirit was through, it flared, then vanished.

Zoe blinked to get her eyes used to the regular light again.

"That. Was. So. Cool!" Jake said. "Where can we find more ghosts?"

Zoe looked at Autumn, thinking she would want the group to help her at Rowan House.

"I think we've worked enough for today." Autumn glanced at her watch. "We better get moving, or we'll be late for our next class."

She chased the others from the storeroom, took the key from Taylor, and headed toward the department office to return it.

Jake smiled at Zoe. "Once a bearcat, always a bearcat."

Zoe nodded. "True that."

✦

*A*utumn closed the door to the music department's office and headed toward the 'A' building and her pattern-making class. She started thinking about what the soldier had said that the others couldn't hear. Olivier. She knew his name. He mentioned her Uncle Theo, who'd worked as an orderly and ambulance driver. But what really got her to take notice was his apologizing for things he had said in his delirium, that she had freed his soul to fly into the night. He was sorry that he couldn't leave his brothers-in-arms behind. He knew she was the one who did it because he was able to smell the same perfume today as he had a hundred years ago. The scent of the release oil.

She knew that Thanatos and Kali had worked with Rose. But how many generations of her family had been working for the Agents of

Death? Was it a family curse? Were any of these people not female or any not named Autumn Rose Cassidy? Kali had mentioned Rose, but not that the relationship went back to before the First World War. Why couldn't she remember if these were things she knew? And why had she felt this pang of sorrow when she talked to Olivier?

She had a lot of questions for Kali after school today, like why her memory still wasn't whole. Death never lied, but sometimes they withheld enough that the truth didn't quite make it through. Autumn hoped that this time, she'd be able to get a straight answer.

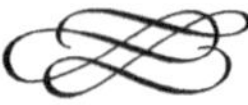

Zoe rode the elevator down two floors in her pajamas and slippers, her backpack on her shoulder. She knocked on Taylor's apartment door.

Nora had gone to work. Saturday was always a busy day at the gallery, especially during the "Fall Foliage" cruise season. And according to her mom, there were three ships expected in at Ville des Saintes Harbor this weekend. Autumn had dodged her calls. She'd sent a text saying she had some work to do, so she wouldn't be meeting with them today. The project still had to be finished.

Taylor answered the door in her pajamas. "You're just in time for pancakes."

"Well, I would hate to intrude," Zoe said, pulling a bottle of maple syrup out of her bag.

Amelia peeked over her daughter's shoulder and started laughing. "Get your purple-pajamaed self in here, Ms. Williams. Breakfast is getting cold."

"Yes, ma'am." Zoe closed the door behind her.

Zoe and Taylor brought all the books into the kitchen. They helped clean up after brunch. Amelia had gone into her home office to get some work done for a meeting she had coming up. Ethan poured himself a second cup of coffee and brought it into the den to watch some TV and fold laundry.

Taylor picked up a book on fairy tales. There were others on folklore and myth. They ranged from anthropology texts to children's picture books.

Zoey pulled out her notebook. "I know this looks weird, but I think I figured it out."

"Figured what out?"

"Autumn's secret."

"You realize you've become obsessed with your cousin. Every time we talk, our conversation drifts to Autumn."

"I need to understand. The soldier's ghost knew who she was. And she recognized him. There's a story there, and I need to know what it's all about."

"Zoe, we have a big project due in a little over a month, and we don't even know what the artwork is going to look like, let alone have anything on paper."

"I know that, but I need to do this. Otherwise, everything I thought I knew about my grandparents is a lie."

"Zoe, no. It's not like that." Taylor hugged Zoe. "It doesn't matter what you read or find out. There's one thing you can believe as the God's honest truth: your grandparents were good people, and they loved you."

"I know." She felt deflated. "Maybe I should put this stuff away, and we'll go over stuff for the exhibit."

"No, you've got me curious now."

Zoe took a deep breath. "I think Autumn and Grandma Rose are the same people."

Taylor dropped into a chair and opened her mouth to speak but couldn't. She took a deep breath. "What?" She looked puzzled. "What?"

"Listen. I know this sounds crazy, but it's the only thing that makes sense." Zoe counted out the facts on her fingers. "In all the papers we looked at, one set of parents, Elizabeth and James, is named. A woman named Kali is always named guardian. And the estate is always left to her namesake."

"But you were there in the hospital when she died. She *died*."

"Maybe she died for a few minutes until her body could heal itself. Then she wasn't dead anymore."

"If she's immortal, how come your grandmother looked old and your cousin looks young?"

"I thought about that. I remembered the Queen in *Snow White*, and how she was able to magically change into the old apple-seller. What if Autumn can do the same trick?"

"You know if we find that spell, we can make it rain money."

"Come on Taylor. This is serious."

"No, it's nuts." Taylor ran her hands through her hair. "If she *is* your grandmother, why wouldn't Autumn know things about you and your mother?"

"But how did Autumn know about Jake's Uncle Walter? And how did she know what an Archie was?"

"If it's true, why on Earth would she decide to go back to high school?"

"Maybe it's so she can get her paperwork updated. I don't know what her thoughts are." Zoe pulled a tablet out of her knapsack. "I scanned all of the photos at Rowan House and put them into chronological order. Each photo set goes from a young teenage Rose to an old grandmotherly Rose, and then the series starts again. Each set spans about fifty years, give or take. I used the layering tool in the photo-retouching program and put one Autumn Rose over another, and their faces lined up perfectly. Even twins don't have the exact same face. But these women, born in different eras, have the *exact same face*."

"That's more than genetics or coincidence." Taylor looked at the photos on the tablet. "What's this around her neck?"

Zoe manipulated the photo to magnify the necklace her ancestor wore. She had seen it before. She scrolled through the photos to see if she could find the necklace again. "It's the same piece in at least five of the twelve photos."

"You think there's some necklace making her immortal?"

"Maybe." Zoe looked off into the distance for a moment. She opened one of the anthropology books and flipped through some of the pages. "Here. This book talks about spells cast on amulets and charms." She put her hand down on the page. "What if the jewelry makes her appear older than she is?"

"Or look younger." Taylor shrugged. "There's no saying how old she looks without her magic. She could look like she's fifty as easily as she could look twenty."

"I never thought of that." Zoe closed the book. "We have to find out how she's doing it."

Taylor stacked the books and put them in the knapsack. "Let's forget this for now and start work on our assignment."

"Tay, thanks for making me feel not crazy."

"Wait for it." Taylor got her sketchbook open. "We still have an installation to create. I think that will make us both plenty crazy."

⁂

Kali got Autumn up early, even though it was a Saturday. Autumn and Thanatos would work downtown again today.

They got into the car. "Today, we go to the train station, *Koukla*. It's a good place to help *Ka* in general. This station is fairly old, so it will also be a good place to clear ghosts."

Autumn asked him to stop the car. "I forgot to put on my jewelry."

"It's okay. Check the glove box."

Autumn opened the compartment in the car's dashboard. There was a small box with her hoop earrings inside. She put them on. She felt a weight in her coat pockets. The two stones had appeared where she would need them. She and Uncle Theo talked about school and the traffic, the weather, and which restaurant served the best coffee.

Thanatos parked the car in a lot across from the train station, and they went inside.

The escalator took them down below the Clover Convention Center. They walked down the corridor, past display windows for jewelry and other gift stores. People walked quickly, eyes forward. Some, in business clothes, headed from the subway to the office buildings that connected the Clover to the underground city. Some carried backpacks or wheeled suitcases, racing for commuter trains that would take them up north, or passenger trains that would take them across Canada or to the US.

Autumn and Uncle Theo stopped in the station itself. Despite all of the activity when they entered the building, the place was relatively quiet. Autumn could smell bacon coming from the restaurants. Music played in the small magazine stores along the walls of the central area. People lined up beside the gates, waiting for their train to be called. An agent removed a rope blocking the entrance to a stairway. People started walking down the stairs toward the platform, while another agent helped a man in a wheelchair into the small elevator that would get him to his train. The agent leaned over and said something, and the two men laughed. Children played with toys or with a parent's phone while waiting for their turn to board other trains.

A two-year-old girl ran past them, her harried father not far behind. The joy was evident in her laughter as her little feet slapped the tile. Autumn couldn't blame her. The corridor was wide, and the marble floors were flat and even. None of the problems a little child would encounter on a sidewalk, none of the dangers of a street. Who could resist running through this huge, echoing space?

"Are you ready to get to work, *Koukla*?"

Autumn nodded and moved through the crowd. A man rushed through the corridor, a briefcase in one hand, a suitcase in the other. Autumn saw that his *Ka* needed to be released. She positioned herself so that he would have to brush by her when he hurried past. Face red and sweaty, he apologized when he tapped her hand. The phone in his pocket rang. He looked at his watch, then looked up at the board to see the train schedule. He wiped his lip with the back of his hand and took a sip from a bottle of water he took from his coat pocket.

Autumn saw Thanatos come up behind him and put his hand on the man's shoulder. He whispered something in the man's ear, but the man didn't move or react. He took a few steps toward his gate. The water bottle slipped from his fingers, and the briefcase fell to the ground. The man clutched at his chest. A woman screamed as he dropped to his knees. A ticket agent and a security guard came running. The agent pulled out his phone as the guard began doing CPR.

She watched as the man's *Ka* took hold of his host's soul, and together they followed Thanatos to a golden doorway that appeared in the wall. The man looked back as the agent paced beside his body, waiting for the ambulance. The security guard continued, although, from the expression on her face, she knew the man was gone.

Numb, Autumn sat down in one of the chairs near a coffee shop.

"So, you want a coffee, *Koukla*?"

She looked up. Autumn had spent so much time with Uncle Theo, the person who told dad jokes and took her for treats. How could she forget who he truly was? He was Thanatos, the Greek embodiment of Death—the one people called the Grim Reaper. Had she ever witnessed him or Kali at their work before?

"Uncle Theo, I don't understand." She pointed back at the corridor, tears in her eyes. "How can he be dead? I just separated him from his *Ka*. Isn't he supposed to get three months to get his affairs in order? How could he die today?"

He crouched in front of her. "I'm sorry, Autumn. I thought you realized that not everyone who is meant to die gets those three months. Just because their *Ka* is still with them doesn't mean their time hasn't come to an end. The two are linked, true. But the two don't necessarily depend on each other."

"I don't understand. Was that my doing? Did my taking his *Ka*, kill him?"

"*Koukla*, you've reattached *Ka*, correct? That shows that a *Ka* can separate from a healthy person. Well, the opposite is also true. A *Ka* can stay stuck to a dying person." He raised her chin. "I think we've done enough for today. Let's go home. You have homework, and I have to go to the store to get the groceries."

She nodded and allowed herself to be led back to the car. This was something she would always remember.

"Thanks for the ride, Aunt Nora," Autumn said as the car pulled up in front of the house. "I don't think I would have been able to get this onto the bus."

"Not a problem." Nora got out of the car to open the trunk and help Autumn take out her sculpture.

Autumn had a large plastic tube on a strap on her shoulder. She stood beside the car. "Why don't you take the portfolio, and I'll carry the hunk of rock? They aren't heavy, just unwieldy."

Nora took the portfolio and the plastic tube and led the way up the stairs of Rowan House. She rang the bell before Autumn arrived next to her.

Kali opened the door. She looked surprised to see them. "My dear Madam Nora, it's so good to see you again. Is there something I can do for you?"

"Helping my niece get all of her artwork and homework delivered to her door."

"You look well." Kali took Autumn's things from her.

"Thank you, Madam Kali. Why don't you and Uncle Theo come for dinner with Autumn tomorrow night? I'm sure Zoe would love to see him again, and you and I can get to know each other better."

"I'm afraid Thanatos and I won't be able to make it. We have a friend's surprise party coming up, and we are part of the planning group."

"Maybe next time." Nora turned and waved goodbye. "I'll pick you up tomorrow at around five."

"That's great," Autumn replied. "Good night."

Kali closed the door as Autumn went toward the stairs to take all of her stuff to her room. Kali stepped in front of her, blocking her path. "Come with me please." Kali led Autumn to the library. "Nora looks well, does she not?"

"She's been doing yoga. Maybe that's why."

"Do you think that's all it is?"

Autumn looked at the floor. "I've only known her for a month. I don't know what she looked like before, so I can't say more than that."

"Stop this nonsense, Autumn Rose. This memory problem you say you have won't work anymore."

"I'm not pretending."

Kali nodded and circled around Autumn. Kali's eyes seemed to grow larger and darker with every step. The library seemed very gloomy like the colors were being pulled out from the objects around her and swallowed whole. The only light in the room came from the burning fireplace.

Autumn went to open the lights, but they were already on. She moved to the window to open the drapes.

"Leave them alone." Kali's voice echoed through the room, coming from everywhere and nowhere. Something about her tone reminded Autumn of the clash of steel.

Autumn waited. Her stepmother used silence as a means of getting confessions from her children. The lack of sound usually caused her stepbrother to want to fill the void and make his mother happy. It didn't take long until he spilled the beans—not only spilled, but he would have those babies soaked, cooked, and canned. He would not only give her a complete play-by-play account of what had earned her stepmother's displeasure but also where everyone had been standing and who'd said what to whom.

It never worked on Autumn. When Death is your godmother, you learn that peace can come with the silence of the grave.

"Nora is on the list, but she still has her *Ka*." Kali circled her as the walls whispered Autumn's name. "Why is that?"

Autumn shrugged one shoulder. She wiped her palms against her jeans. "I must have forgotten my tools at home and didn't notice."

"Enough!" Kali slammed her hand against the desk. "You were set with a task."

"She was doing a headstand in her yoga class and your image was by her shoulder. I swear."

"Enough!" The fire expanded until the flames appeared to fill the room. But the room didn't get hot, and nothing burned. Kali stood in the flickering red light. Her skin began to change from her usual warm human tones to a deep midnight blue, dark as the night sky.

"Auntie-ji, I'm sorry. I got confused." Autumn's heart pounded. "It's my memory. I must have forgotten what I was supposed to do. I'm sorry." The energy in the room made the hair on her arms and the back of her neck stand up. Kali's sari vanished in a puff of smoke. The skulls of Kali's necklace moved. Those with eyes sought Autumn out. The blood from Kali's skirt dripped loudly, matched only in volume by Autumn's harsh breathing. The bones in the severed hands of Kali's belt cracked and popped as they tried to claw their way to safety.

This was the Goddess her mother met in the jungles of India. The room was stifling. Autumn couldn't breathe.

"Please, Auntie-ji.". Something warm ran down her legs as her bladder gave way. Autumn ran for the door. Her shaking hands couldn't grip the knob or get it to turn. She pounded on the door; her screams frozen in her throat.

Her knees gave way, and she slid to the floor. She lay by the door, sobbing. "I couldn't do it! I couldn't do it! Not again! I killed the two men I cherished most in the world. I couldn't kill my daughter too."

The French doors flew open. Kali was gone.

"Not again," she mumbled. "I couldn't do it again."

Autumn wasn't sure how long she lay there. Thanatos whispered something in her ear as she was wrapped in a warm quilt. Someone picked her up as if she were a small child and carried her up the stairs.

"Come, little one," Oya said as she helped Autumn undress. "Let's make you feel better."

Autumn couldn't answer. Her tears had left her vision blurry, and she wasn't sure if she would ever stop shaking. Over and over, she mumbled, "I loved Olivier. I loved Eddie. I loved them both, and I killed them both."

Oya helped Autumn into a warm bath. The water smelled of lavender. "Breathe deeply, Precious. You'll feel better."

"My mother was a real bearcat. A true badass." Autumn leaned back in the large tub, feeling sleepy and a bit drunk. "Alone in the jungle at night, sick, and she sees..." She chuckled, humorlessly. "I see the same thing. And I fall apart."

Oya patted her hand and poured scented water into the tub from a ceramic pitcher Autumn had never seen before. "You are in a better state than most. And your mother wasn't braver than you. She wasn't thinking about herself. She was thinking about the safety of her child."

"The safety of my child." Autumn closed her eyes. She felt like she was walking through a dream. Oya helped her from the tub and wrapped her in a fluffy towel. She was then enveloped in an oversized velour bathrobe that still smelled of Eddie's cologne.

Oya tucked Autumn into bed and closed the door behind her. She walked down the stairs. Thanatos sat in the kitchen, staring into his coffee cup.

"You ought to be ashamed, the pair of you." Oya looked at the ceiling. "You can't hide from me, Miss Kali." She stood in the center of the floor, her fists on her hips. "You fetch yourself back here now, Old Woman, or by all that is holy, I will go out and find you myself."

Kali came in through the swinging door. She was no longer the avenging Goddess, just beautiful Auntie-ji. She brushed past Oya.

"Is she all right?" Kali poured herself a cup of tea.

"Old Woman." Oya sucked her teeth. "You went too far this time."

Thanatos grunted. "She is right. A thousand percent right."

"There are rules," Kali said, "and she must follow them."

"Are you about to lecture us on following the rules, Madam? The godmother of a mortal woman?"

Kali turned on her heel and left them to go stand outside Autumn's bedroom door.

utumn tossed and turned in her sleep. The potion Oya had put into her bath was trying to bring her a peaceful rest, but her mind had other plans.

In her dream, Rose and Eddie were at their country house in Eastern Canton. She, as Autumn, could only stand by and witness. The house looked the same, but some of the furniture was wrong. There were pieces from her father's house in Kent: the stone fireplace, the set of teak boxes her father had brought from India, and the portrait of her mother, Elizabeth.

"Rose!" Eddie called from the other room.

Autumn felt afraid. She had to leave. The front door seemed miles away. The floor looked normal, but it felt like she was moving through mud with weights strapped to her ankles.

"Autumn Rose?" Eddie called. "Where are you?"

She wasn't herself anymore. She was Rose. She closed her eyes and whispered, "Please, please, please, don't let them find me." Autumn Rose fought her way to the door. Sweat dripped down her back with effort and the blazing heat of summer.

Autumn finally opened the door. A blizzard raged outside. She sensed someone in the room with her. Eddie appeared out of thin air. Kali crouched on the floor in front of him.

Eddie reached for her hand. Kali blocked him. "*Beti*, Eddie's not yours anymore. He's gone." She stood up. "You helped him leave, remember?"

"I didn't! I couldn't!"

"Maybe you're not thinking of Eddie at all. Maybe you're remembering someone else."

Eddie melted away, and Olivier stood in his place. "It's okay,

Archie. I was ready." He took her hand. "We discussed it. I knew what was going to happen, and I was ready."

"I didn't want to. You know that."

"We know, Autumn Rose," Olivier said. "I loved you. The only thing I wanted was for you to have a happy life, even if it was without me." He turned, letting go of Autumn's hand.

Eddie moved past Kali. "I was ninety-eight percent sure of what you were going to do when you got into the car. I thought there would be time. I didn't realize how ill you were, and that I wouldn't be able to help you when the car went off the road." He took both her hands in his.

"I never wanted you to die with me." She looked up at him. "I couldn't..." A sob caught in her throat. He was the same young man who ran into her sewing room. She blinked. He was Eddie on their wedding day.

"Dance with me, Rosie." Then he was the businessman, the artist, the father of a teenage daughter. He smiled. Their song came on the radio.

"Won't you dance with me, Rosie?" Eddie bowed. Rose curtsied her reply. Not the deep curtsy of her youth. Her old knees couldn't do that anymore. Eddie took Autumn Rose into his arms, and they began to sway to the music. Just like they had on the morning of the accident.

They talked and laughed, and the look of love in Eddie's eyes… She knew she would free him from the role of nurse and caregiver, free him to live out his life, and she would be free of the cancer and the pain. She would free them both by going over the cliff. She would do it alone.

"There never was anyone for me but you." She lay her head on his shoulder.

He chuckled. "And I couldn't stay here without you. You know that."

They whirled around the floor. In the dream, Nora and Zoe were watching them, smiling, applauding. Neither of them noticed Kali moving toward Eddie.

Autumn broke from the dance. "No!"

"You can't challenge me," Kali said. "You're not your mother."

"But I never tried to challenge you. I never asked you to spare my life," a soft voice said. Autumn turned. Elizabeth was no longer in the painting. "I never fought you for my life, Death. I never asked you to save my daughter. I called on you to *defend* my daughter."

"I don't understand," Autumn said to her mother.

"My darling, I was the one who was dying, not you." Elizabeth glared at Kali. "But if Madam Kali or any of her cohort had come for you, I would have fought them like a tiger. No matter how horrible her countenance."

Kali changed into the Goddess Autumn had seen in the library. Elizabeth held Autumn by the shoulders and looked into her eyes. "I am not a badass." She turned Autumn around so she could look at Kali. "Are you willing to challenge Kali's authority over you? Will you fight for *your* daughter?"

Autumn woke up. It was dark outside. The house was quiet. She stared at the ceiling. How was she going to save Nora?

Nora, her daughter. Not her aunt, her very own little girl. Today and forever. And she would fight for her.

*A*utumn hung up the telephone. She had let the school know that she wouldn't be there today. She'd used the same excuse she'd given to cancel her dinner with Nora. It had been a very tearful weekend.

The secretary heard Autumn's tear-stained voice and thought she had a terrible cold. The woman was very sympathetic and told her to rest and drink lots of fluids. She also reminded her that if she would be away longer than three days, she would need a note from her doctor.

Three days. She had three days to re-evaluate her whole life. No, that was wrong. She had more than one life to try to integrate.

She remembered her life with Olivier, her first human love. And she remembered his death. She remembered Eddie and their life together. All her memories came flooding back in a torrent that threatened to drown her.

She was Autumn Rose Cassidy, Daughter of Major James Cassidy, retired, of the East India Company, and Elizabeth Marie Grail Cassidy, of Kent, England. Autumn Rose was born in 1848, in the British colony of Bombay, India. Which meant that at the end of October, she would be one hundred and seventy years old. No candles on the cake, please. The fire department has rules about that kind of thing.

In the vast span of her life, she had been a lady of leisure, a landlady with a pub, a shopkeeper, a nurse, a philanthropist, a costume designer, an artist, a wife, a mother, and a grandmother. But she had always been an Agent of Death. She had always worked for her godmother Kali Ma, the Hindu Goddess of Death. Death had been a part of her childhood, her teenage years, and all four of her incarnations.

Autumn only had one life when she was a baby, living with her mother and her father. Her stepmother had been part of that life, as had the estates she had inherited. The land in Ville des Saintes had been part of her father's retirement settlement. She'd built Rowan House a lot later.

She poured herself a cup of tea and took it upstairs. Thanatos had to pose as her son so she could get the place built. As a woman, she didn't have much status, and the tradesmen didn't trust her opinions. But her son was able to get everything he wanted, even though the money was hers. This century seemed to be much better. So was the last century... well, the end of it, anyway.

Olivier Calvert. He had worked as an accounting clerk before the Great War. One day, he was telling stories about his home in Nova Scotia and the people he knew there. And then, he was gone.

Olivier, Edward, her parents, her stepfamily, her neighbors, her friends. They were all gone. She started to cry again, even though there couldn't possibly be any more tears left.

Kali knocked on her bedroom door. Autumn had locked it and didn't answer her call. "I've left some food here for you *Beti*. Whenever you're ready."

Autumn listened for her footsteps on the stairs. She lay down on the bed and stared at the ceiling. She had no idea what she was going to do with the rest of this life, knowing what she knew. Feeling like she did. If she died today, would she wake up again, in this bed, with no memory of Nora or Zoe or Taylor or Saint Katherine's?

Would that really be such a horrible thing?

$\mathcal{Z}$oe rang the doorbell. School had ended for the day. The sun seemed to be going down earlier now. This time of the year was hard. The dull light made everything feel blah.

She and Taylor waited for someone to answer the door of Rowan House.

"Looks like nobody's home," Taylor said.

"Autumn's supposed to be at home, sick. So, unless she's at the doctor, somebody has to be here." Zoe tried the door. It was unlocked. "That's very weird. This door is always locked."

"What if they're waiting for an ambulance?"

"Someone would have answered the door." Zoe opened the door and walked in. "Hello! Autumn!" She pulled Taylor inside and closed the door.

"This place is giving me the creeps," Taylor whispered as she followed close behind Zoe.

There wasn't any noise. No one was walking around. There was no hum of an appliance. No television or radio playing. Not even the sound of muffled voices behind a closed door. It was like the house had no life left in it. It hadn't ever felt this eerie, even after her grandparents' funerals. Zoe turned suddenly and came nose-to-nose with Taylor.

"We have to go upstairs to the bedrooms," Zoe said.

"That's fine. I'll wait outside." Taylor started to leave. Zoe grabbed the back of her jacket. "See, Zoe. This is where the smart people leave the haunted house; before the axe-murderer comes out of the secret door in a Halloween mask."

"There are no murderers. Besides, didn't you like visiting the ghosts in the music room? If there were any ghosts here, they would be my grandparents' friends. And they were very cool artists. If you saw one of those ghosts with a sheet over their head, it would be more of a performance piece than wanting anyone hurt." She pulled Taylor toward the stairs. "Let's go."

They made it as far as the master bedroom. The door opened; they jumped. Autumn stood in front of them in her bathrobe and slippers. "What the hell? Are you trying to give me a heart attack?"

"No," said Zoe. "We rang the bell, and no one answered." She looked Autumn up and down. "You look terrible. Do you have the flu or something?"

"She's been crying," Taylor said as she put her arm around Autumn's shoulder. "What's his name? We'll go beat him up for you."

A faint smile played across Autumn's face. "Thanks Taylor. It's not that. It's a little hard to explain."

"Try," Zoe said. "We're listening."

"I'm going to be leaving Ville des Saintes."

"Just like that?" Zoe said.

"What about our project?" Taylor said.

"What about our family?" Zoe said. "We were finally becoming friends. We were doing cool stuff. And you're just going to leave?"

"I can't explain more than that. I'm sorry."

"No, you're not sorry! You got us to believe in you. You got Rose's money. So, you're off to scam some other family?"

"Zoe. You wouldn't understand. It's all for the best."

"I had this weird idea that you were Grandma Rose... I mean, more like Rose than this. Come on, Taylor. We have to go tell Ms. Bridges we're back to working on our own." She started down the stairs. "Have a nice life, Autumn Rose."

Zoe pulled Taylor behind her as she ran down the stairs, and slammed the front door behind them. She felt her knees getting weak. Taylor sat on the stairs beside her and held her while she wept. "How could she leave me again? She wasn't even going to say goodbye."

Taylor shook her head. "That proves that she can't be your grandmother. The car crash was an accident. I'm sure she would have said goodbye if she'd had the chance." Taylor sighed and let Zoe lean her head on her shoulder. "Autumn is your cousin, but that's all she is. You can't choose your family. If they become your friend, you get a lucky break. If not, well, they just become a name on the family tree."

Zoe nodded and pulled a tissue from her pocket. "Let's go grab the bus and get some hot chocolate at the Timmies near the McCord."

"Sure. It will give us a chance to discuss our project and check out the guys from the university."

"I love you, Tay. Always looking for the rainbow and the farting unicorns."

Taylor pulled Zoe up off the stairs, and they walked arm and arm to the street.

*A*utumn went into the library and turned on the computer. Her cell phone rang. Without looking at it, she shoved it into the drawer.

Now that she remembered her life as Rose, she knew the password for the cloud account that had all her properties listed, as well as her personal bank accounts and investment files. Her will listed some of these, but never the full extent of her holdings.

Kali had been right. She didn't need to go to school or work. She had enough money for several lifetimes. She would live out this one as she had her previous lives: alone. Husbands and children were complications that she didn't need. The lesson was learned and wouldn't need to be repeated.

The house's landline started to ring in the hallway. Autumn Rose let it ring.

Eddie had been an experiment. A wonderful, fun, exciting... experiment. She stopped herself from going down that rabbit hole again. She missed him, but that was only a human reaction. He finally knew who and what she was. That was why his ghost didn't even try to contact her anymore.

The house in British Columbia was rented and would be for

another two years, as was the house in Jamaica. The one in Kent was vacant. She scrolled through the list. There was a cottage in Maine that she hadn't been to for a while. Maybe they could start there if Kali was willing and her passport was ready.

There was a commotion downstairs. Someone was running through the house, shouting her name.

Zoe flew into the library. "You have to come quick! There was an accident at the gallery. Mom's been hurt. She's on the way to the hospital."

"There's nothing I can do, Zoe."

"Please! I need you. I don't have anyone else."

Autumn nodded and closed the laptop. "Uncle Theo will drive."

hanatos stopped at a light. Zoe hung up her phone. "Taylor and her parents will meet us at the hospital. I don't understand why I had to call them."

"And I don't understand why you didn't. We are going into a hard situation. It's important someone with a clear head be available."

Zoe nodded. "When my grandparents died, Madam Kali came to meet us. We weren't sure who she was, but she knew who we were. She told us that she had been close to Rose."

"Really?"

Zoe nodded. "After they were gone, we walked into the waiting room, and she was there. She introduced herself and got everything organized. She helped Mom call the undertakers and everything. She might seem very strict, but she can be very caring."

Autumn thought back through all her lives: her early days after her own mother was gone and the frosty relationship she had had with her stepmother. Kali Ma had been there for her, and Autumn had broken her one rule. Nora deserved to clear up all the things she needed to, to die without regret. Autumn Rose had given that gift to so many people over the centuries. She could have given her daughter that one last gift.

She caught Thanatos' eye in the rear-view mirror and tapped her ear. He nodded and continued driving down the street.

"When did you put on those earrings?"

Autumn reached up. She was wearing the gold hoops. Her seatbelt felt a bit snugger when the stones appeared in her pockets. "I've been wearing these for days. They must have been hidden by my hair."

They pulled up in front of the hospital and found Nora in the intensive care unit. The nurse let them go in together to see her. Nora's eyes were closed, and she had a breathing tube in her mouth.

Kali floated above Nora's feet.

A doctor walked into the area and motioned for Autumn and Zoe to follow him. "Are either of you her daughter?"

"I am. This is her niece."

"Are either of you over eighteen?"

Zoe and Autumn shook their heads. "I see." The doctor looked down at his chart.

The elevator door opened, and the Mains rushed to where Zoe and Autumn stood. Ethan put his hand on Autumn's shoulder and looked into Zoe's face.

He turned to the doctor. "I have Ms. Sterling's Power of Attorney." Amelia hugged Zoe and Autumn. Taylor put her arm around Zoe's shoulder. Ethan pulled a document from his briefcase.

"Perhaps we can talk over here." The doctor led Ethan away as he read the document.

"Zoe? Are you okay?" asked Taylor.

"I don't know. I don't feel anything." She looked at Autumn, wanting an answer.

Ethan and the doctor returned. The doctor nodded and continued to the nursing station.

Ethan led the girls to some molded plastic chairs. He stopped to collect his thoughts. "Zoe, your mother sustained some injuries when the shelving unit fell, but they aren't serious. The shock of the accident aggravated the heart problem she's had for many years. One of the valves that regulate the flow of blood through her heart appears to have been damaged some years ago. Apparently, the heart valve had been leaking for some time, and it was beginning to fail. The accident added to the strain so the valve stopped working. The doctor wants to go in and replace it with an artificial one."

Amelia hugged Zoe harder.

"What did you say?" Zoe asked

"I told them to go ahead."

Autumn felt her eyes begin to tear up. Nora would go through open-heart surgery, and it wouldn't make a damn bit of difference. Kali was at Nora's feet. She'd be dead before the day was out. The hospital walls were closing in. "I need to get some air."

She went to the area near the elevators and stared at the soda machine.

"Can you help her?" Zoe was standing behind her.

"I don't know how I can help."

"It's just... I saw all this stuff about Autumn Rose Cassidy, and I thought... if they're you... if you are all the Autumn Roses, then..." Zoe became frustrated. "If you could give her a transfusion, so that she becomes like you, so that she becomes a young person again. Or lend her your magic amulet, so that she can't die."

"Zoe, I don't know what you're talking about." Autumn's heart beat so loudly, that she was sure it would break. "There's nothing I can do." She started to walk away.

Zoe grabbed her arm. "You have to do something!" She moved closer, so she could speak quietly. "You can't let your daughter die."

Autumn searched Zoe's fear-filled eyes. She took her grand-daughter into her arms and let her sob. Elizabeth had faced Kali to save her daughter's life. Autumn Rose could do no less. She was her mother's daughter.

Autumn held Zoe at arm's length. "It's time to collect yourself, Zoe baby. Your mother will still have to have the surgery. I can't fix that. But we can ensure the outcome. We'll have to work quickly."

Zoe nodded. They asked Taylor to follow them into Nora's room. Most of the machines and intravenous bags were on wheels, which would help. Autumn checked that the bed was also on wheels.

"We have to turn the bed around," Autumn said.

"Why?" asked Taylor.

"It's something she learned in India," Zoe said. "It's like Feng Shui, only different."

Taylor shrugged. "If it helps. Which way?"

Autumn pointed to the corner of the bed. "Release the lock on the bed's wheels. Each one has a lever. Find them? You'll each be responsible for moving one of the poles as we turn the bed. I'll make sure the breathing tube stays secure."

Autumn waited. "Are we ready? We'll have to turn everything pretty quickly." She counted to three, and they carefully turned the bed.

Kali was at Nora's shoulder. Autumn took the reattach salve from her pocket and spread it on Nora's cheek. Her *Ka* remained the same. It was still prepared to leave.

"It didn't work," Autumn said. "What did I do wrong?"

Thanatos appeared in the corner of the room. "She's dying, *Koukla mou.* Fixing her *Ka* won't change that."

"But there has to be something I can do!"

"Who are you talking to?" Zoe asked.

"Thanatos. The one you call the Grim Reaper. He was the family's driver."

"The man who works in your house? Uncle Theo?" Taylor looked at the wall Autumn was talking to.

Autumn put more of the potion in her hand and gave some to Zoe and to Taylor. Zoe gasped. Thanatos stood beside the bed in a long black robe, a golden glow around his body. He seemed a lot younger than when he pretended to be Autumn's driver. A scythe hung from his shoulder.

"Uncle? Theo?" Zoe said.

"It's still me, Zoe *mou.* I still like coffee and ice cream sundaes with chocolate. I just have another job on the side."

"What can I do?" Autumn said. "I have to help her."

The orderlies came into the intensive care unit to take Nora down to the operating room. They watched the bed pass through the sliding door. "Uncle Theo. Please."

"I'm sorry, *Koukla*. This is what must be."

They shuffled from the room. Taylor ran to her mother and cried on her shoulder. Her father fought back tears as he rubbed her back.

"I thought you might need me," Kali said as she reached for Zoe's hand. Autumn paused. Kali nodded. The three sat together on horrible plastic orange chairs, holding hands. "And now we wait."

Zoe stood at Nora's bedside, holding Autumn's hand. Nora's face was swollen. The breathing tube was still in her mouth. The tape holding it in place distorted her features. There were wires and tubes connected to various places on her body. Machines surrounded her, beeping, and blipping as if they were trying to comment on the case in front of them. They'd dimmed the lights in intensive care, which made Nora look even further away from this life. Tears collected on Autumn's lashes. Zoe stroked her mother's hand, but Nora didn't open her eyes or react.

"I can't simply stand here," Autumn said. "I have to find a way to fix this."

"How?" Zoe asked.

Autumn stuffed her hands into her pockets. She felt the bottle of release potion and pulled it out.

"Wait!" said Zoe. "Doesn't that stuff make ghosts go to Heaven or something?"

Autumn nodded.

"You can't use that on my mother!" Zoe stepped between Autumn and the bed. "I won't let you."

"I'm not. I have an idea." Autumn left the room and headed to a chapel she had seen near the elevators. She walked through the chapel to a balcony.

Zoe followed her. "What are you going to do?" She held out her hand for some of the oil. "Let me see too. Please."

Autumn poured some of the release potion into Zoe's hand and some liquid into her own. Then she added some of the reattaching potion. She took Zoe's hand in hers and waited. Ghosts walked past them from all directions. Zoe pressed close as some of them still displayed their injuries. "Autumn, what are we doing?"

"I'm waiting for someone." She looked around. Nora wouldn't go to the afterlife by herself. No one ever did. A golden door appeared in the wall behind them. It opened, and Edward Sterling stepped onto the balcony.

"Grandpa!" Zoe gasped.

"Zoe baby? How come you can see me?"

"Hello Eddie," Autumn said.

"Rosie. Lovely as ever." Eddie's smile said it all. "Did you like our conversations at Rowan House?"

"I did. And I missed you when you stopped playing with the radio."

"You were doing well without me. It was hard for me to see you and not be able to be 'us' anymore. You not recognizing me was breaking my heart."

"So, Grandpa is going to take Mom with him?" Zoe's eyes filled with tears. "They'll be together at least."

"We're still waiting for more people." Autumn looked around at the cityscape. The lights of Ville des Saintes started to come on. "I know that you're around, ladies. So, you might as well show yourselves."

A young woman in a white dress came toward them. "You are a very unique individual, Autumn Rose Cassidy. You are the only person who can give Fate a headache," Clotho said as she led Lachesis and Atropos onto the balcony.

"I've been waiting for you three." Autumn turned to her family. "Zoe, Edward, these are the Fates, Clotho, Lachesis, and Atropos. They're going to help me save Nora."

"We're going to do *what* now?" Atropos asked.

"Nora is my daughter. Her spark of life is failing. I want you to give her mine."

"Rosie! What are you doing?"

"Saving our daughter, Eddie."

"We can't do that," said Lachesis. "We have an arrangement with Kali, and…"

"Kali!" Autumn called. "I need to speak with you, please."

Zoe clung to Autumn's arm as soon as Kali appeared. Her face was dark. Her lips were blood red. Skulls hung on a chain from her throat to her waist.

"That's not Madam Kali," Zoe whimpered.

"What do you wish?" Kali's voice was deep and smoky.

"It is Kali. Oh wow!"

It was hard to look at Kali that way. Autumn took a deep breath. "Auntie-ji. Will you please let me go on? Break the bond with the Fates, so that I can give my spark of life to Nora."

"But why? Haven't I been a good godmother?"

"Oh, Auntie-ji. You've been the best godmother a girl could have hoped for. But I don't belong here anymore. I went through a lot of years, doing what I could to help you. I had a taste of humanity when I met Olivier. But I never knew what it meant to be a human until I discovered my love for art, married Eddie, and we created our family."

"I kept you living."

"But they gave me a life."

"Are you sure?" asked Clotho.

Kali said "No," at the same time Autumn said "Yes."

"Autumn, *Beti*, you're in shock. The memories and Nora's illness..."

"Kali, I have never been so clear in my life... any of my lives. Please, ladies, can it be done?"

Atropos spread out the tapestry to see where Autumn Rose had rejoined the timeline in this incarnation. "It's possible. There would be differences in Zoe's future and in some of the people Nora would encounter with this new path, but nothing drastic."

"Auntie-ji, please. Let me do this. I want to give my life to my daughter, so she can see her daughter grow up—like I did. Meet her grandchild, like I did. And maybe fall in love again and have a love like I had."

"You peeked," giggled Lachesis. Clotho rolled her eyes.

"You're not supposed to tell," said Atropos.

Kali turned on the Fates, her eyes blazing. Zoe gripped Autumn tighter.

"This is your fault!" Kali shouted. "You put him in her path! You gave her the child. That wasn't part of our agreement!"

Atropos crossed her arms. "Look, lady. You asked us to keep Autumn Rose alive and allow her life to restart whenever she died. And we did. But we weren't going to change Edward's life and destiny to suit your whims."

"We controlled her destiny for you," said Lachesis, "just as you asked."

"You said nothing about the destinies of those she would meet," said Clotho.

"They are pretty heavy into the semantics," Edward said. He winked at Zoe and wrinkled his nose the way he did when she was a toddler. "It's an 'immortals' thing, I guess."

Zoe calmed down. Autumn could feel the circulation return to her arm.

Kali paced in front of them, her skirt dripping blood as she passed. Zoe pressed her lips together. She was looking a little green, and Autumn could feel her tremble, but she refused to release Autumn's hand, and she didn't run away. There was her mother's Grail Cassidy magic in her granddaughter after all.

Kali turned, her countenance returning to the Auntie-ji Autumn and Zoe had always known. "Autumn Rose, I swore to your mother that as long as you behaved to my standards, I would not take your life or your soul."

"But you aren't taking my life. The spark will be with Nora, where she can use it. And as for my soul, it's going to be with Edward."

Kali took Autumn's face in her hands. "If that is what you wish. If it's what will make you happy, I won't stop you. And now, my sweet girl, I must be on my way."

She stroked Zoe's cheek, smiling sadly. "What? Why?" asked Zoe.

"It's time. We were trying to live among mortals, like mortals, and that time has passed." She turned around. "Thanatos, are you ready?"

"Almost, my friend." Thanatos came in through the wall. Several souls followed him. He pointed toward the golden door. The men and women looked a little nervous. There were shouts and whistles as if a party had started on the other side. The souls looked happy and surprised and ran through the door into the waiting arms of their friends and families.

"It was a working visit." He shoved a travel mug into his jacket pocket.

"My Zoe." Thanatos kissed her on both cheeks. "I expect great photographs from you, *Koukla mou.*" He pinched her cheek.

"Will I see you again, Uncle Theo?"

"Yes, but not for a very, very, very long time."

Thanatos took Autumn's hand in his. "*Agape mou*, my little love. Be happy." He kissed her on the cheek. "It was my pleasure knowing both of you." He put two fingers in his mouth and whistled.

A horse, pale as moonlight, stepped gingerly out of the night. Uncle Theo passed through a shadow and came alongside the horse. He was shrouded in a black cloak, a scythe hung over his shoulder, his face now that of a skull.

Thanatos, the Greek Shephard of the Dead, son of the Goddess of the Night, called to them, "Remember, my precious Zoe." His horse danced in a circle. "You won't be able to see me, but I'll be watching out for you and Nora. I love you both, my darling *Kouklas.*" The horse reared, then galloped away.

Autumn fought to control her sobs. Kali held her close. "Come, come, my sweet girl, all will be well." She lifted Autumn's chin. "You know most people cry when they see death coming, not when they pass them by."

Autumn laughed through her tears. "Auntie-ji, I will really miss you. I owe you so much."

"Nonsense," Kali said. "It was a lot of fun."

Kali kissed both girls. As she stepped away from them, she changed. Her skin turned midnight blue, and her arms multiplied. Her sari was the white of those in mourning. She drew a short sword from the scabbard at her hip. "I will always love you, my sweet *Beti.*" She rocketed up into the air.

Autumn searched the sky, trying to see which star had once been her godmother, her Auntie-ji, Kali Ma, the Hindu Goddess of Death.

Zoe put her hand on Autumn's shoulder. "Are you okay?"

"I don't know." She pulled a crumpled tissue from her pocket.

Eddie cleared his throat. "Can we get back to business, please?"

Clotho stepped closer to Autumn. "This isn't going to hurt." She passed her hand through Autumn's chest. She pulled out a small ball of pure white light.

"It's beautiful!" whispered Zoe.

"Remember that. Always," Atropos said as they walked into Nora's room.

Clotho held the spark above Nora's chest. It floated above her hand. When Clotho took her hand away, the ball sank slowly into Nora.

Zoe looked around at all the machines. "Nothing's changed."

"You might think so," Lachesis said, "but now she'll get better."

"That was so incredible!" Zoe turned to Autumn. Her mouth dropped open.

"What's the matter?" Autumn asked.

"You're Rose again. I mean, you look like my grandmother, not my cousin."

Autumn peeked at her reflection in one of the metal trays waiting on a table. She was an old woman again. And that was perfect. "Now what?"

"We have reset this timeline," Lachesis said. "Once you and Eddie go through that door, people here won't remember ever having met you as you are now. To everyone, you will have died in the car accident. This body will never have been created."

Autumn Rose nodded. A strange knowing came over her as she saw the way things were changing. She hugged her granddaughter. "Zoe, I'm so happy I got to know you as a friend. And I'm proud to be your grandmother." She leaned over and kissed Nora's cheek. "Keep well, my little love. Stay strong, and I wish you both a magical life.

"Before I forget." Autumn ripped off the end of an opened box of bandages and wrote a note on the piece of cardboard. "You'll find my copy of the new will in the middle drawer of the desk in the library. The one the lawyers had will never have existed because I wouldn't have needed it for this incarnation." She looked at the Fates, who all agreed. She gave Zoe the cardboard. "This is the password to the files on the portable hard drive attached to the laptop in the library. It will show you all of the properties and things that you and your mother have inherited from the Cassidy family."

Zoe looked at the cardboard and put it into her pocket.

"Goodbye, Zoe baby," said Eddie. "You're destined for great things." He polished his nails on his chest. "You come from great stock."

"Can I hug you, Grandpa?"

He opened his arms, and she gave him one last big bear hug.

"Are you ready, Rosie?" Eddie offered her his hand. Somewhere behind the golden door, a song started to play. It was The Beatles, singing *In My Life*. It had been their wedding song.

"Dance with me, Rosie."

"Always and forever."

Edward took Autumn Rose into his arms, and together they waltzed through the golden door.

"One more time around the floor? Really, Mom?" Zoe said.

Nora held on to the IV pole as they strolled past the elevator and approached her hospital room. "The big anniversary is so close, I can feel it. I intend to be at every single event, especially your installation. Let's go."

Oya Bridges poked her head out of Nora's room. "Don't overdo it. You won't build your strength back up in a day."

"One more round. I'm tired, but I feel great. Does that make sense?"

"Perfect sense." Oya offered Nora her arm, and the three walked around the floor.

Zoe glanced over at the woman she once knew as her eccentric art teacher. She and her mother were walking with a Goddess. Wrong word—Oya was an Orisha, who could read minds, apparently, or so the smile she flashed Zoe led her to believe.

Once the doctors said they would be moving Nora into a regular room, Amelia and Ethan had insisted that Zoe come back with them to their apartment to get some rest. But Zoe said she wanted to go to Rowan House first.

She'd gone into the house, asking that they wait for her in the car.

The key had appeared on her ring after her grandparents had moved on to the afterlife.

Taylor and her parents didn't remember Zoe having a cousin Autumn. But she knew the truth. She went into the library, found the will and the hard drive, and packed it and the laptop into her grandfather's briefcase that stood by the leg of the desk, just as he had left it when he went to Eastern Canton the weekend he and Rose passed away.

When they got back to their apartment building, Zoe wanted to go to her own home. She was exhausted and wanted her own bed.

The house had looked exactly as they had left it that morning. She searched for the lawyer's letter about Nora's long-lost brother. She found it, but it was different. The letter she found mentioned Eddie's estate, but there was now a second paragraph stating that they had found a separate will filed by Autumn Rose Cassidy Sterling. Rose's will said that the entire estate went to Nora. They asked for more information, so they could put together a final report of the Cassidy holdings. Taylor showed up at her door about five minutes later, ready to come in for a sleepover.

Zoe adjusted Nora's hand on her arm as she felt her mother tiring. "Mom, I found something at Rowan House that I think you should look at," Zoe said when they made it back to the hospital room.

Oya and Zoe helped Nora back into bed. She opened the laptop.

"It's locked," Nora said when she saw the icon for the portable hard drive come up on the screen.

Zoe turned the computer so she could see the screen and typed in the password she had gotten from Autumn. The hard drive started to hum. File after file opened on the screen. There was one called 'Rowan House', another for the building their condo was in, another for a house in England, and another for houses and properties in the US and the Caribbean.

One folder had a list of names and contact information for accountants, lawyers, and property managers, as well as banks and account numbers.

"I got Uncle Ethan to call the lawyers in the letter. We printed it all out, and he brought them the hard copies yesterday."

Nora studied the screen, shook her head, and stared again. She smirked, then started to giggle. "It's a good thing my heart was fixed." She laughed "This might have stopped it."

"So, we're rich?"

"Yes honey. Your grandmother came from a long line of careful investors. We are more than rich. We are stinking rich." Nora grinned wickedly. "And your father can't touch a flippin' dime."

Zoe and Nora entered the school's Sterling Art Gallery. The place was packed with people. Zoe greeted her fellow students and their parents. She also recognized some of her grandparents' friends and customers. The school's executives fell all over themselves to be introduced. These were the movers and shakers of the art and business world. To Zoe, they were the same, kind people who had visited her mom in the hospital and showed up for her first exhibit in Rose and Eddie's living room.

The Main family came over and offered hugs. Ethan took pictures of everything, but Taylor and Zoe were his stars.

Jacob and Joshua came to extend their congratulations. Jake offered Zoe his arm to escort her around the exhibit. The twins did their installation on two actors who had broken into television on a science-fiction show that had become a cult phenomenon. Their art was not only well received but was noticed by some of the television people Zoe's grandparents had known.

They continued through to the exhibit that had been given pride of place in the whole gallery. The school's gallery curator had moved the photo of her grandparents from the spot in the gallery's doorway to Zoe and Taylor's installation.

The girls had decorated the space with three tapestries. The first was a representation of the house her grandfather had grown up in. The second was the Taj Mahal. The third was a theatrical stage, complete with costumed characters. The tapestries framed a couple who danced in the center of the installation. Zoe printed photos of her grandparents' faces on fabric and quilted and embroidered over the prints to create the couple's heads. Her grandfather's body was made from wooden logs, an old tuxedo jacket, and papier-mâché. Her grandmother's body was an antique dressmaker's form with long opera gloves for arms, stuffed so they could embrace her partner. A purple bejeweled fascinator sat on top of her head.

The couple was secured to a turntable, so they could waltz in their space. A series of songs played as the figures danced, songs that Zoe had heard them sing or play over and over in the car. The recordings crossed eras, languages, and genres.

Nora leaned closer to see the label describing the piece. It was called *"Dance with Me, Rosie"*.

"Isn't it a wonderful piece?" Autumn Rose said as she hovered a little above the floor.

"The girl's got talent," Eddie replied. "She gets it from my side of the family, you know."

Autumn Rose looked over Eddie's shoulder and the the three Fates watching their granddaughter. She caught Lachesis's eye, and the spinner of souls winked at her. "Eddie," Autumn said. "I think there's a lot of my family there too." Eddie smiled and kissed her cheek.

Zoe turned when she heard their voices. She couldn't quite see her grandparents' spirits, but she knew they were there. Because that's where they would always be, watching over her and her mother, just as they had always been.

The End

# WOULD YOU LIKE TO SEE WHEN THANATOS BECAME UNCLE THEO?

Autumn Rose lives in Victorian England with her Godmother, Kali, the Hindu Goddess of Death.

When Kali has to be away from home, she asks Thanatos if he can babysit.

The task should be easy. She's a child. What could possibly go wrong?

https://dl.bookfunnel.com/c9pocfntzt

# ABOUT THE AUTHOR

Judie Troyansky learned at a young age that stories are a type of magic; to take something invisible from one person's imagination and transmits it to another. And so, she became an author.

She lives in Laval, Quebec, with her dog, Buddy. She's been reading tarot cards for more than 40 years, and has been involved with many different forms of occult and esoteric studies.

She can be reached through her website www.judietroyansky.com . There you can subscribe to her newsletter and read her blog, *The Bohemian Storyteller*.

9 780099 515444